THE WHARF AT PORT TOWNSEND BAY

38-MCCU

THE WHARF AT PORT TOWNSEND BAY

Calmar A. McCune

To order additional copies of this book, contact:
Xlibris Corporation
1-888-7-XLIBRIS
www.Xlibris.com
Orders@Xlibris.com

I

In the morning, when the whaling canoe set out, the fog appeared to be thinning, but once away from the beach and upon reaching the outer edge of the kelp, the fog thickened. Moist pillows and banks of fog bunched up, moving off the open Pacific Ocean, over the kelp beds and up into the dripping spruce trees at Cape Flattery. The Makah chief in the stern stated it was too foggy to go further offshore. He directed that the canoe be paddled over the kelp bed, where traction between the bottom of the canoe and the floating bulbs of kelp would keep the canoe from floating away. The six men sat there, waiting. Swells raised the entire kelp bed and the canoe and then moved ashore, causing the men to drop down into a marine valley until the next ocean wave. They could hear the waves that had passed breaking up in a surf line. The wind that pushed the fog made no sound. Once in a while an Indian would hear a seabird flying nearby. Below the canoe kelp stems dropped down twenty feet to anchor-like holdfasts on the ocean floor. Within the kelp forest thousands of small fish schooled about. On one kelp stem just below the canoe an Indian noticed clinging there a large spider crab.

In 1869 there was no United States Coastguard cutter to protect the Indians from people opposed to whale hunting. The protestors were not even within 100 years of being born. The water around the canoe did not include the raw sewage from Victoria, B.C., nor the tons of pollutants carried down the Fraiser River, as would occur years later. The carcinogenic chemicals to be spilled into the waterway from Tacoma, Washington, had years yet to make their debut. No helicopters with a Seattle television crew chopped and whirled overhead to record the movement of the canoe.

For hundreds of years the Indians had harpooned gray whales. In the spring of each year, in small groups, like two to five whales, as many as 18,000 whales would swim from Mexico north along the coast line to the Bering Sea. The warm waters of Mexico served as a birthing place. The frigid Alaskan waters provided food. Possibly, thousands of years ago the two locales were closer. Changes of climate and the shifting of continents may explain why the whales would migrate many thousands of miles.

The Indians heard to the south a "Kwhoooshing" sound and then several more. They knew that in a moment some whales would be passing by. The fog prevented the Indians from chasing the whales. In a while the fog thinned. The Indians could see the surface for about a quarter mile radius.

"Whale!" shouted the bowman. He had seen to the south a mammoth body slide up to the surface, exhale, inhale, and then slide underwater. He suspected other whales were there. The chief directed that the canoe be paddled free of the kelp and into the anticipated line of passage for the whales. At the bow the harpooner stood, ready. At the stern the chief held his steering paddle, prepared to position the canoe next to any emerging gray whale. Mid-ship, the crew double-checked the spruce root lines that ran from the harpoon tip to the sealskin floats. Another crew member prepared to jump overboard. His job would be to swim to the harpooned whale to sew its mouth shut. Air kept in the lungs of the whale created buoyancy that kept the whale from sinking. As they waited the shore-bound fog thickened and rolled over them once again.

Their silent world changed very dramatically, for ten feet away the water parted as a whale surfaced. The chief's instructions brought the canoe alongside the exposed back of the whale. There was no way the harpoonist could miss. He held the harpoon high overhead. The crew expected to see him hurl the harpoon into the body of the whale. They knew the whale would dive, harpoon stuck to its side, pulling the rope and the seal floats. Eventually the whale would tire and it would be then that the canoe would move in for the final kill. But the harpoonist did not hurl the harpoon. He stood there, as though paralyzed or catatonic or a bronze statue.

"Harpoon!" yelled the chief. Nothing happened. "You idiot!" he continued, "toss that damn thing." The bowman did nothing. He just stood frozen. The whale curved down, disappearing into the depths. The last sight of the whale was its tail, lifting out of the water as though waving goodbye. "Idiot! Fool! Idiot! Fool! Idiot!" shouted the chief. "Why did you wait?" The furious sternsman and the curious crew looked to the harpooner for an explanation.

In response, the harpooner lowered the harpoon. He turned and tried to speak, but his mouth was full of vomit which burst out onto the head of the nearest paddler. That second person became nauseous. Then the others did, too. The chief, being heavy-set and immobile, bowed his head and vomited onto his chest. Candlefish that he ate for breakfast, now chewed, rested on his outer garments and glinted their disarrayed silver sides.

The chief realized the fog carried a stench. "Ugh!" he snorted in disgust. "Let's go for shore." Pretty soon the swells took a steeper turn. The chief waited until there was a lull in the surf and then he commanded his crew to paddle hard. The canoe rose, appeared perched on the steep side of a breaking wave. Then it broke free and commenced to surf on the wave's inclined face toward the beach. People waiting on shore hoped to process a dead whale. "Why are you back so soon?" one asked.

The chief explained. "We almost killed a whale. Right there. But a putrid smell came over us. Something is rotten further out at sea. Really bad, like dead humans. Maybe there is a canoe out there floating with dead from another tribe."

The other Indians thought the explanation made no sense. They started to chuckle and then to laugh. Just then the thick fog embraced them, introducing to the shore Indians what the canoeists had inhaled. The entire group became sickened and lost their most recent meal. After that no one made fun of the whalers.

II

The shore wind carried its foul smells up into the forest. The people on the beach dispersed, many of them walking back to the tribal community at Neah Bay. Small, unpainted planked houses adjoined one main street. An open area nearby served as a communal area, especially on occasions of visits by other tribes, when rows of low banked alder fires cooked flanks of salmon. Along the top edge of the beach stood pole rocks that supported overturned canoes. Along the sides of the canoe hulls ran lines of shallow cavities denoting where the builder's adze had chipped away the cedar wood. A few canoes remained upright on the beach, ready to use.

Off the beach, in the bay, a tug had been at anchor for two weeks. The Snohomish was big for its time. Its length was 120 feet; its beam, 15; and its propeller's diameter was 6 feet. The tug assisted sailing ships by towing the ships to and from the constricted inland waters. At the time, the Snohomish was the most modern tug on Puget Sound. Its boiler was heated by coal instead of by endless cords of wood. It was so modern that the Indians were intrigued when first observing the Snohomish move. Being paddlers and sailors, they could understand how a vessel moved by stern or side paddle wheels, but with the Snohomish's propeller being out of sight, underwater, there was a mystery as to what made it move.

Ocean swells curved around Cape Flattery, lifted the tug, and while lowering the vessel moved on to the beach. Sometimes the anchor line would tighten up as the waves tried to take the tug along. When the waves made a small surf line along the beach, pebbles would be pushed about, and as each wave receded the stones would make a clicking sound in the descending foamy jumble. The high tide line along the beach hosted a running line of heaps of rotting kelp mixed with bark, wood, and dead crabs.

The sailing ship the tug was to meet had not appeared. It was two weeks overdue. During those fourteen days crew members, in rotation, had stood watch on the bridge deck of the tug to listen through the fog for a horn or a deck cannon. Nothing sounded. Once in a while the door to the burner would be opened and enough coal would be shovelled in to keep the fire going, but the heat was not enough to build up steam in the thick iron water-filled pipes that crossed the top of the burner box. The crew consisted of a captain, a second mate, two deck hands, and an engineer. When the tug was underway the engineer remained below, mothering the steam engine and bossing the deck hands to shovel coal. The second mate, Bill McNulty, mostly took the helm and performed whatever the captain, Doug Barry, requested.

"Fifteen two, fifteen four, and a pair makes six," counted the captain, and he moved his cribbage peg. Bill counted his cards: "Fifteen two, and a run of three for five, last card, for six." He reached over and moved his peg forward. Their cribbage board was of black slate, argillite, as black as its peg holes. At one end of the heavy board the body of a frog was carved. At the other end an ebony raven looked up. The game board had been made by a Haida Indian and traded to Barry the year before.

"Where are the crew?" asked Barry.

"Janson rowed ashore for groceries. Derek is on deck doing watch in his own way."

"'In his own way,' what do you mean by that?"

"Well, he's sitting on the stern rail fishing."

"For what?"

"Ratfish."

"It's your deal. Why ratfish?"

"I asked him that and he said he has Scandinavian neighbors who boil ratfish liver to render out its oil. The oil is used for lubricating tools and as a massage oil."

The captain evaluated his hand, repositioned his cards, discarded two cards to add to a crib, and then said: "I hope he does his rendering away from the tug. Years ago I tried to render ratfish to extract oil. The smell was bothersome and seemed to attract every rat in the area."

The two counted their cards and moved the pegs anew. The second mate asked: "Where is that darn ship? What's its name?"

Without taking his eyes off his newly dealt cards, the captain replied: "As to your first question, I have not a clue. Regarding your second question, the ship we are waiting for is called the China Princess."

Bill McNulty glanced out a porthole, as though expecting to see the ship, and said: "I'll be glad to see it. Impossible to sleep, what with sea lions barking all night—and those tribal drums banging late." The captain took his eyes off his cards for a second and looked at the second mate: "It is noisy here. What bothers me about this anchorage is the uncertainty of the weather. If we get a storm from the north then this little bay offers no protection. The anchor will drag and we will be beached.

"Bill, what's the engineer doing?"

"Disassembling steam gauges and cleaning them."

In a while Janson rowed back to the tug. He passed the groceries up to Derek. They hooked ropes to the stern and bow eye bolts of the rowboat and then the two men pulled on a rope that ran through two pulley blocks. The ropes grew taut. Slowly the rowboat lifted off the water. The men kept pulling on the rope and the craft rose twelve feet above the surface of the water. Then Derek pulled another rope that moved the lifting boom and the rowboat directly over the stern cabin roof. They let some of the rope out and the boat sank into its resting mounts. Janson took shorter ropes and lashed the rowboat down. Then, after stowing the groceries in the galley, Janson sat down and watched the cribbage game.

After a while the captain asked Janson: "Any news from shore? After all the drumming last night to prepare for a whale hunt, did the Makahs score a whale?"

The crewman told what he had heard on shore: "Hunt was a bust. Some strong smell in the fog blew onto the whalers and they got sick. Stench followed them back to the beach. People waiting on shore became sick, too."

The captain and the second mate glanced at each other. One of them asked Janson to repeat what he had just said.

So," reflected the captain, "something is out there. Dead whale? Canoe full of dead Indians?" No one said anything. The captain stared over his cards and looked lost in thought.

"Look," he said, "for two weeks we've been sitting here, bored stiff, waiting. We could steam up, pull anchor, go west and then south around Cape Flattery, and then when we encountered the smell we could turn upwind to discover the source of the smell. Probably a dead whale that did not sink. We know the currents around here and we can easily navigate by compass—so we can find our way back through this fog. Shall we go look?"

No one said anything. He was the captain.

"OK, tell Derek to stop fishing. You," he said looking at Janson, "and Derek can shovel a couple tons of coal into the burner. Steam should be up in two hours. By that time, the engineer should be ready."

Doug Barry walked just to the left of the five foot diameter wooden-spoked steering wheel. There, he yelled into a speaking tube: "Bridge, to engine room." He heard an acknowledgment from the other end. "We are going to steam up and pull anchor in two hours. OK with you?"

"Ya, Captain. No problem."

"Thank you," replied the captain.

The new coal blanketed the old fire and for a few minutes it looked like the flames were smothered and extinguished. Thick smoke issued from the stack. Then the heat from the pre-existing fire ignited the new coal and the flames lit up the interior of the burner box. The new brightness cast illumination out through the burner door causing the engine room to appear less gloomy. The flames licked up around the many pipes that contained fresh water.

Upon being heated to 212 degrees Fahrenheit the liquid boiled. The boiling produced steam which had no place to go except along the pipeway to a series of controlled vents, one of which released steam to the open air. Another vent released steam into a chamber where the increasing pressure would move a piston head away, down a cylinder, until another vent caused that steam to escape. Then the piston head moved back up the cylinder until forced to retreat, again and again. Attached to the cylinder head was a piston rod eight feet long that extended to a large flywheel. The boiler pressure gauge moved from zero to three pounds pressure, then ten, then on up to 120, at which point the engineer pulled a cord that rang a small bell at the bridge, signalling that the steam was up.

At the captain's command, steam was side-vented into a two inch diameter iron pipe that ran forward to the bow winch. That winch consisted of a smaller steam engine that was geared down to turn a capstan. As the anchor chain came aboard, its clanking and clunking sounds competed with the hissing escapement noise from the little steam engine. When the anchor broke surface, Janson turned a valve to stop the steam engine, which, in turn, stopped the capstan from turning. With a pike pole he jabbed at the anchor to dislodge bottom gunk that had caught on the anchor flukes. Then he moved the valve to introduce steam back into the engine and the anchor rose from the water to its hanging position. There, Janson ran cross-lines to secure the anchor. He turned to the bridge and yelled: "Anchor up."

The captain moved a brass lever from its stopped position to forward quarter speed. Belowdecks, the engineer opened valves and pulled some levers. Boiler steam within the pipes gushed into the foot-wide chamber of the piston head, pushing the head away. The engine room was alive with sound. Rays of light from air entry holes in the burner wall danced about the room. The steam engine's long piston arm moved back and forth, slowly turning a huge flywheel attached to the main shaft. Needles jiggled on different pressure gauges.

When the engineer pulled a six-foot lever to engage the turning flywheel to the propeller shaft, the entire tug shuddered and then moved. The captain glanced astern and saw prop wash forming. They were underway.

The tug skirted the shoreline west. Then it circled Tatoosh Island and ran south along the coast line. The captain kept a good distance from shore. Being within fog, there was no shore to see. He relied on his charts and his compass.

"Bill," asked the captain, "help me here. Let's open some bridge windows and the two side doors. We'll just let the fog roll through the bridge. If there is a smell, we'll inhale it."

In about ten minutes, the captain and the second mate grimaced at each other. Quickly they turned the tug to run upwind and closed the windows and the doors. The stench accomplished its introduction. That smell was so bad the captain suggested they go 90 degrees southerly until the air cleared and then go upwind. That done, the second mate took the helm. The captain walked outside. He climbed a steel-rung ladder to the roof of the bridge cabin. Then he ascended a rope ladder up the mast to a cross arm. There, he straddled the spar, hugged the mast and looked forward into the fog. Behind him he could hear the steam exiting the exhaust stack: kwish, kwish, kwish, kwish. Thirty minutes went by. Nothing happened. The tug cut through the fog. Overhead the fog thinned enough so that when the captain glanced upwards he saw blue sky. After a while, the captain and the upper mast were in clear air. Lower than that, the rest of the tug moved encased in fog. Looking back, Barry could see clearly the top of Mt. Olympus. He looked north and observed the tips of the mountains on Vancouver Island. To his left, south, he noticed an undulating line in the sky and watched for a short time before realizing it was a formation of migrating geese. The V line intersected with the route of the tug and passed overhead. Barry could imagine the cackling gossip of the geese, but the sounds of the venting steam blocked out the honking. With binoculars he scanned the horizon. Not much could he see: blue sky over a blanket of fog.

The day was fairly calm. No wind. No cross-chop. No whitecaps. From the west came ground swells that had originated days or weeks before, hundreds of miles away, in what had been a fierce storm. The storm was long over, and the mellowed waves marched across the Pacific as a final announcement of what had been. These residual waves raised and dropped the Snohomish. The tug advanced up one wave while the vessel leaned to starboard, then on crossing the crest of the wave, it leaned to port as it descended down the backside of the passing wave. Where the captain perched, the lurching was more pronounced.

In a few minutes he looked through his binoculars again. Nothing caught his eye. Just an expansive field of fog, slowly evaporating under the sun's heat. He did notice on the horizon one place where the fog bank had a hump. Ten minutes later he looked again. He saw nothing new, except when he looked at the hump he noticed what to him appeared as toothpicks or denuded trees sticking up out of the mound of fog.

"Something, but what?" he wondered. Shortly he looked anew. This time he could clearly make out four masts. The upper cross spars were mottled with white. He removed a shoe and let it fall onto the bridge roof. Out popped Bill McNulty to see what was up.

"Ship adrift!" yelled the captain. He gave the second mate a direction by pointing his arm toward the ship. McNulty ducked back into the bridge and as he turned the helm, the captain saw the bow swing to its course. Now the tug was on a direct approach to the ship ahead. When the fog thinned enough to see the ship from the bridge, the captain climbed down the ladder, retrieved his shoe, climbed further down and took over the helm. As he steered he kept the tug free of being directly downwind.

"Let's come up on the stern and get the name of this vessel," he said to McNulty.

When the tug came within two hundred yards, the captain signalled the engine room for a reduction of shaft RPM. Then he pulled a cord and held it down for seven seconds. The pulling on

the cord moved a lever that had obstructed the flow of steam to
the three-chime whistle. A low, melancholy, mellifluous steam
whistle hooted through the fading fog and wrapped its vibrations
throughout the sailing ship. Instantly, the patches of cotton white
on the spars expanded in size and took flight. The captain said:
"Seagulls. Must be hundreds of them." Only the birds acknowl-
edged the presence of the Snohomish. No one appeared on the
deck. The ship clearly was adrift. Its masts slowly pitched with the
passing ocean swells. It was not underway. It had no wake. The
long bowsprit extended out from the foredeck and from it rope
stays ran up to the forward mast. Along the sides of the ship,
shroud lines angled up each mast. Ropes went everywhere. Most
of the sails were wrapped and secured. A few remained unfurled
and dangling.

Slowly, the tug positioned itself near enough to the stern of
the four-master to see the transom board. There, carved in a thick
panel of wood, a band of broad gold paint around its perimeter,
they could read the ship's name: China Princess.

"OK," commented the captain, "we have our ship. Let's board
from the windward side."

III

Janson came up from the engine room to see what was going on. The captain turned to him and said, "Please break out four shotguns. Load them. One is for me. One for McNulty. Janson, you keep one and stay on the bridge cabin roof. Derek will take the helm and he shall retain a shotgun within easy reach. Once McNulty and I board, please reverse the tug at least thirty feet out away."

Against the side of the sailing ship the tug looked small. No welcome ramp or ladder extended down from the high coaming. Barry jumped down the tug's bow onto the side of the ship. Grasping shroud lines he climbed up to the ship's coaming, then he swung his legs over to be fully on board. On the tug, McNulty made certain each gun was on safety—he gently tossed one and then the other up to Barry. Then, he, too, jumped across and climbed the lower part of the rigging. The tug pulled away.

"Captain," exclaimed McNulty, "I landed on a body!" Barry made no reply. He held his shotgun ready with its safety off. His attention was drawn to the many human bodies that covered the decks. The foredeck, the mid-ship deck, and the stern deck lay covered with contorted bodies. Those bodies with heads up had their eyes pecked out. He saw near him a cadaver with an open mouth and he observed that the tongue had been chewed out. In some bodies, knife holes appeared as black crevices in white shirts—and what must have been bright red blood that once ran and pooled on the deck had dried and turned black. Knives protruded from some bodies—and when the captain withdrew one knife he recognized it as being made of bamboo.

Gingerly, the two men stepped over and between the lifeless

forms and walked to the bow. They advanced down a ladder into the crew's quarters. Sunlight revealed a forecastle that was crowded with dead, decaying bodies. When McNulty moved the leg of one body in order to get by, dozens of beetles fell from the clothing and scampered across the floor into shadows. A dry death smell was the only welcome the two men received. They shortly returned to the main deck.

The number of bodies increased toward the stern. The two men expected someone to greet them, but no one did.

"Look," the captain said, using the barrel of his shotgun to gesture toward the back of the ship, "does it seem to you that all those bodies piled up by the door to the stern cabin suggest they were trying to get inside?"

McNulty looked and said, "Yes, do you see how the bullet holes in the stern cabin door splinter the wood outwards? That means the shots were from the inside of the cabin. Besides, I see no firearms laying around here."

"So," picked up the captain, "only those inside had firearms. Was there a mutiny? Suppose people are alive in the cabin?"

McNulty bent over the bodies and asked the captain, "Do you notice that the dead are Celestials?"

"What does that word mean?"

"Chinese."

The captain bent over and looked at the corpses near him.

"Yes, right."

They both realized they would have to move a pile of bodies before they could access the stern cabin door. They leaned down and pulled and rolled bodies. When the door became accessible they pushed. It would not budge.

Barry walked to the side of the ship and yelled to the tug to pass over a fire ax. The tug approached. A fire ax exchanged hands. The tug drew back.

McNulty swung the ax onto a panel of the door. The oak panel did not collapse. After he had axed the door for several minutes, the captain took the ax. When he swung a panel fell inward.

With the ax he cut away a cross board just below the new hole. In a moment he broke off an upper door hinge. The two men reached forward and pushed inwards. The top half of the door collapsed. They could then see why the door had not opened, for just inside the door an oak table had been placed on its side and pushed up against the door. Because the interior air smelled so foul the two men waited several minutes outside for fresh air to enter through the doorway. They listened for sounds from the room but heard nothing. Sunlight revealed beyond the barricade a row of bodies. Next to two of the dead were rifles that leaned against the over-turned table. McNulty entered the room, examined the rifles, and told the captain that the weapons remained loaded. "No shortage of ammunition, I guess," he said.

"Stand-off," the captain said. "Must have been a stand-off. People outside trying to get in, and officers and crew inside trying to keep everyone else out. These people are not Chinese. They look European, probably English."

McNulty moved to the back of the cabin and noticed leading from there a second door. He turned to the captain and said, "This door, do you suppose it leads to the captain's quarters?"

"Check it out," replied the captain.

McNulty turned the door handle and twisted it. Without protest, the door opened. The two men observed a luxurious room. On the floor rested a bright, flowered Persian rug. The walls consisted of panels of polished, varnished cherry wood. To one side there was against the wall a bed that had walnut railing on the outer side to prevent the captain from being tossed from the bed in a storm. A set of windows allowed the two men to glance out over the water beyond the stern of the ship. Just before the windows and resting partly on the rug was a mahogany desk. On its far side sat a man whose body leaned out over the desk. The captain jostled the arm of the sitting person. "Dead," remarked Barry. "He's been so for a long time."

From the other side of the desk, McNulty said, "Look, captain, is he resting on something, a book maybe?"

One of them tilted the body backwards and the other reached and pulled away what appeared to be a large book. Then the body was gently lowered back to its initial position.

Barry carried the book to a window for better light. On the book's leather front cover he read: "Ship's Log. China Princess."

With the air too uncomfortable—and with much to do—he carried the log with him back to the tug and then gave orders to place the sailing ship under tow. From the stern of the tug, Derek passed a thin line to Janson who stood on the bow of the sailing ship. Janson pulled in that thin line until a heavier line attached to it came onto the China Princess. He passed that towing line through a hawser and secured it to the bow anchor post. He stepped over and around bodies when he made his way to the stern of the sailing ship where he turned the steering wheel until the rudder was in line with the keel, then he lashed the wheel to retain that alignment.

As the tug moved away, a tow line ran off a huge stern reel. First 110 fathoms of Manila line ran out, then 30 fathoms of wire cable. From the tug's stern the tow line disappeared underwater and re-appeared before the bow of the sailing ship. Finally, with no further line being unreeled, like a horse being pulled by a halter, the ship turned slowly and fell in line behind the tug. The Snohomish ran up two flags. One flag signalled that the tug had a tow. The other signaled "Emergency. Keep away."

By now the fog had vanished. Dark green forests of Vancouver Island and of the Olympic Peninsula stood in clear sight. An outward-bound sailing ship came into sight. It lay becalmed. "Too cheap to hire a tug," the captain muttered. When the Snohomish steamed by it a quarter mile off, Barry used his binoculars to look closely at the other ship. He observed a Canadian flag and he noticed several people on the stern deck staring back at him with their elbows raised as they looked through their own binoculars.

"That second flag may have them curious," he remarked before turning the helm over to the second mate. He walked to the stern and lay down in a hammock near the cable drum. It was not the safest place to be, for if the tow line snapped, part of the cable could backlash up over the stern and injure him. He felt safe enough. The weather was kindly. What little wind there was came off the stern at about the same speed as the tug, so for where the captain was the air stood still. Patches of loose kelp and air-chambered seaweed floated by totally inert until kicked apart in the boil of the prop wash.

Douglas Barry lay in the hammock. His head rested propped up on a pillow. He took the log and opened it. The first page of the log of the China Princess read:

IV

Ship's Log—China Princess—Volume Five

June 19, 1868. London. Ship provisioned. Cargo on board and battened down. Crew assembled. Hoping new cook is better than last one. Lines taken in at sunset. Fell away with the tide, reaching Graves End at dawn.

June 20, 1868. Crew rowed Emily and our two kids, Sparry and Ebert, ashore. Now, outward bound for Bombay to deliver ammunition and office desks.

June 21, 1868. Fair weather. Following sea. Wind at ten knots. Under partial sail until crew becomes familiar with vessel. French coastline visible to port. Leaving English Channel. New cook, Ah Tso, is excellent. For lunch he prepared pickled pig's ear. Sauce tasty.

June 22, 1868. Twenty knot wind off port. Ship heeling some. Crew appears capable. Routine replacement of rigging has commenced. Should take about a week. Then will examine all stowed sails for rot. Today Ah Tso prepared for dinner wild duck marinated in orange-juice vinegar. Delicious.

In chronological order the log showed entries for each day. The tugboat captain flipped along the next pages, noting references to the China Princess making its way along the African coast, stopping for provisions at Capetown and then sailing on to Bombay where it unloaded and took two hundred British troops and thirty horses on board to transport to Calcutta. At Calcutta, several hundred 200-pound hemp sacks of opium came on for delivery to China.

Douglas Barry skimmed on through the log, seeing as yet no explanation for the crisis that befell the ship.

April 4, 1869. Hong Kong. Cannot unload until customs bribed. Took three hours to negotiate. Opium will be unloaded this night. Then must lay at anchor for four days to accept new cargo.

April 8, 1969. Hong Kong. Took 198 men on board at noon. All from one village. Evening, took 201 more men on board, all from another village. Ship ready to sail come morning. Passengers are traveling to United States of America to construct train tracks.

April 9, 1869. Underway. Slight sea. Barometer falling. Passengers are very quiet. Food excellent, except when Ah Tso attempted to serve pickled kitten.

The tug boat captain skipped on ahead.

April 23, 1869. Things not going well. Passengers no longer submissive and quiet. Instead, the passengers are spitting at each other. They yell at one another in a manner suggesting intended violence.

April 24, 1869. Conditions bad. Passengers are clearly hostile to one another. Not certain why. Requested cook, Ah Tso, to talk with passengers. He reported back that a mistake had been made in selecting the passengers. He explained that for over a hundred years feelings of hatred and enmity existed between the occupants of two closely-located villages. When people from one village encountered members of the other community, arguing and name calling would commence and it was not uncommon for fighting to take place and for someone to die. At one time the imperial government stepped in and built a high stone wall between the two communities. The cook explained that the mutual hatred remains. "Bad blood, bad blood, bad blood," he kept repeating.

April 25, 1869. Ship course due east. Full sail. Pulling nine knots. Wind off starboard stern. Barometer steady. Crew reports increased tension between passengers.

"Something's about to happen," speculated Barry. He read on.

April 30, 1869. Morning. Body of passenger found on deck. Bamboo knife jammed into his heart. No one accepts blame. Two hundred miles east of Strait of Juan de Fuca. Making seven knots.

Afternoon. Organized a meeting in cabin. In attendance sat a spokesperson for each village. The cook, Ah Tso, interpreted. I told the two villagers of the importance of getting along. I told them we are close to landfall. The two spokesmen said nothing. They sat with their eyes focused on the floor. Outside the cabin, the passengers waited in silence. The men from one village clustered on the port side and the other villagers stood in silence along the

starboard rail. They all stared in-expectation at the open doorway
of the stern cabin. I asked Ah Tso to get from each spokesperson
some assurance that there would be no further violence. In Man-
darin he spoke to them. They just sat there, making no reply, still
looking down at the floor. A long silence followed, broken only by
the creaking noises of the ship's hull. Slowly, almost in unison,
their eyes moved across the floor to the feet of the other. Then the
eyes looked up to the knees, then to the waistline, then to the
shoulders. When their eyes met, simultaneously, each screamed in
hatred and rushed at the other. Each held overhead bamboo daggers that had somehow been hidden within their apparel. The
knives could be seen being thrusted again and again into the fighters. As they fought they rolled out the door. Ah Tso followed,
trying to get the fighting to stop.

When the two camps of villagers saw the fighting, a roar went
up, hidden weapons appeared, and the two groups rushed each
other. Ah Tso ran between them, trying to keep them apart. The
merging fighters engulfed him. He fell and was trampled. The
ship's crew gathered in the stern cabin. We closed, barricaded the
door. Thuds and screams could be heard outdoors for what seems
a prolonged period of time.

May 1, 1869. Fighting continued all night. Moments of quiet,
then shouts and screams. At three in the morning, a fight took
place overhead on the stern cabinroof. The roof was like a drum
skin, and it seemed as though the cabin were within the drum.
Each time a body hit the stern deck the impact made a loud noise
in the cabin. Impossible to sleep. We could actually listen to the
fighters breathing. Finally, the frantic movements became fewer,
and then there was the sound of a heavy body falling on the roof.
Whoever had not fallen grabbed the head of the downed person
and banged it against the overhead stern deck, time and time again.
Then we could hear someone walking away and there were no
further sounds overhead.

May 2, 1869. Ship no longer underway. Crew, reluctant to perform duties, remains in stern cabin. At dawn I armed myself and two crew and we opened the cabin door. It looked like one side had won, but nothing was certain. Bodies lay on the deck, some moving a bit. We needed food and water. When we walked across the deck to the galley we discovered that the food reserves had been tossed overboard. The water barrels had been drained. Clearly, there is now limited food on board and no water. Hopefully, we will encounter a passing ship. On our walk back to the stern cabin, our way was blocked by passengers. They stood and stared. I tried to wave them to one side but they remained. Then one of them spoke and they moved one step towards us. We took several steps backwards. He spoke again and they took another step. Most alarming. From the sleeves of their shirts they drew out bamboo daggers. I instructed the crew to be ready to shoot. I told them that when I gave the command, to shoot as many passengers as possible that stood closest to the port rail. Quickly, I aimed at the one who had spoken and yelled "Fire!" The guns blazed. Several passengers went down. We edged by those remaining and ran for the cabin door. No sooner than were we inside than hands pounded on the door. Doing some damage to our ears, we shot through the door. It took two shots to make a hole in the thick oak door paneling. By the time the pounding stopped our room was filled with smoke from the discharge of the guns.

Then, "whammm," a thunderous sound occurred as the passengers rammed the door with a gaff boom. Clearly, it would not take long to break down the door. The ram struck again and it looked like the door might give. A crew member moved right behind the door and looked through some of the bullet holes already there. Then he fired through a hole. He must have hit a passenger for we could hear a painful cry. The crewman kept a lookout through the door holes and each time the boom was picked up he fired. Eventually, efforts to ram the door ceased. Fortunately, there is ample ammunition in the stern cabin. Some food here, but no water. Even though there are fewer sounds on the deck we are afraid to leave the cabin. A standoff, of sorts, is taking place. I am worried the ship may be torched.

May 3, 1869. Standoff continues.

May 4, 1869. Ongoing standoff.

May 5, 1869. No noise on deck for a long time. Two crew, Henry Hanks and Charles Baird, insist on leaving cabin to look for food and water. They stepped out at one in the morning. No moon. We re-barricaded the door and waited for their return. In just a few seconds after the cabin was secured we heard screams. "No! I cannot swim!" someone yelled. We realized the two crew members were being tossed overboard. From the water they yelled for help, but there was nothing we could do. Eventually a slight wind blew the ship away from the drowning men.

May 6, 1869. Standoff. We are getting weak.

May 7, 1869. Food gone. Ample ammunition but afraid to leave cabin. One by one the men near me are dying. Sort of a gentleman's death, just being in a chair and passing on. I suppose I, as well, will be passing on.

That marked the final entry in the log. Douglas Barry closed the book and returned to the helm. He suggested to the second mate that he read the log. "Without any reason, people can sure hate one another," he commented as McNulty accepted the book.

When the Snohomish pulled the China Princess by Port Angeles, people on Ediz Hook peered through telescopes and saw the flags flying. A telegraph message transmitted to the quarantine station at Port Townsend read: "Diseased ship under tow your way."

The quarantine master, concerned as to what contagion might be afloat, hired out a small steam launch. It took him from Point Hudson out around Point Wilson, then west along the high banks of North Beach. He crossed the entry to Discovery Bay to Dungeness Spit. There the launch waited. A little speck to the west became larger and taller. Eventually, when the tug and its tow were nearby, the steam launch drew up alongside the Snohomish. Briefed by Barry, he took possession of the sailing ship log.

"Continue under tow," he directed Barry. "When you reach Port Townsend Bay drop anchor anywhere that you are not upwind of Port Townsend. If the wind changes, then relocate. I will meet you about midnight to take the bodies off. Please keep your crew and anyone else off the sailing ship." With that said, he reboarded the steam launch and made for Port Townsend. Barry directed that the towing cable be brought in to half-length.

Upon his return, the quarantine master set to work. He commissioned a tug and barge to be ready for departure near midnight. He sent word to Fort Townsend for ten volunteers. When the men arrived he had them cut old sail canvas into three hundred squares of seven feet. He hired a teamster to bring two tons of lime down to pile onto the barge. Quickly, he read the final pages of the ship's log to confirm what Barry had disclosed. Then he had the log sent to the Port Townsend Chief of Police.

At midnight, when the barge came alongside the China Princess, pitch torches were tied to the rigging and lit. The flickering flames revealed to the newcomers the tumble of dead bodies. Lime was shoveled into buckets and the buckets were passed from the barge onto the sailing ship. From the buckets the lime was sprinkled over each body before the cadavers were rolled onto canvas squares. Then the canvas was flapped over the deceased. Ropes were passed around the open ends of the cloth and cinched tight. Two soldiers lifted the wrapped body to rail and rested it on the coaming to get their breath. They pushed the body onto a steep wooden ramp that allowed the body to slide down to the deck of the barge. There, two other soldiers grabbed an end of the canvas wrapping and moved it onto an orderly pile at the opposite end of the barge. Each worker wore a perfumed bandanna. By two in the morning all the bodies had been found, wrapped and stacked. From the distance of the tug Snohomish the barge appeared as though it carried cords of wood.

The quarantine master cleared the tug to continue its tow on to Seattle. At three the barge reached the quarantine station. A carriage with two horses in front waited there to take the bodies of the captain and the crew to the mortuary.

The question arose as to where to take the remaining bodies for cremation. The quarantine master had his own solution. For years his wife had nagged him about a small ravine on their property. In order to have more garden space she wanted it filled. Now, he saw a chance to end her annoying pestering. He knew that rainfall collected on the neighborhood slope and ran down the ravine, but he felt the flow was nothing to worry about. To satisfy his wife the quarantine master said: "Borrow the mortician's flat-bed carriage once he is done with it. Take the bodies to my home. Next to my house runs a shallow gulch. Just roll the bodies into that depression and then place about four feet of dirt on top. Shovels are in the barn." Before dawn the work was done.

When the bodies were tumbled into the ravine and then covered with dirt, there was no way to distinguish who was from which village. The cadavers, encased in soil, lay at random. Over time, each body decayed. Skulls collapsed. Rib cages fell apart. Bones softened and became as soil. Each deceased human diminished in size as it rested within its fungus-coated canvas shroud.

In a few years the home of the quarantine master became

vacant, stayed that way for twenty years until it was purchased by a pharmacist who remodeled it for his family. The new owners had no awareness of the impromptu burial. Eventually, no one in Port Townsend remembered just where the bodies were placed. A few old-timers insisted there'd been a cremation, using beach logs as fuel.

Sandy soil above the dead men allowed the rain to seep down to the bodies. But just below the canvas coffins, a horizontal layer of clay extended to the bluff and blocked further downward passage of water. Instead, the rain water ended its downward movement and as seepage advanced along the top of the clay sill to the bluff. There, the moisture dripped and fell and formed a small creekway. In summer, along the face of the bluff where the seepage descended, brilliant green watercress grew in clumps. Some winters, during a deep freeze, the water froze, forming long icicles, giving the bluff there the appearance of glistening fangs.

By 1944 the town experienced many economic ups and downs. Hopes for Port Townsend to be a major railroad terminal had come and gone. Dreams of being the key city to Puget Sound had long faded as Seattle and Tacoma grew in population and in commerce. A Port Townsend pulp mill did employ over 350 people. An active military fortification was busy at the edge of town. The large Victorian brick buildings downtown, built by Eastern money years before, remained, as did many of the old wharves. South of Port Townsend, near Quilcene, logging of second-growth trees kept several logging companies at work.

Where the ravine had been, the collapse of the bodies caused subsidence in the ground which, in effect, re-created the earthly depression. New rainfalls and snowmelts eroded some of the topsoil. In a few more years some of the decomposed bodies would have been exposed, but in 1944 Port Townsend street department obtained council approval to place a sidewalk there, running from the street, over the ravine, to the edge of the bluff. It connected to a new cement stairway leading down the face of the bluff to reach downtown. With the new stairway, people could walk to and from the downtown streets. Uphill from the bluff, rainwater that fell in the area still collected and ran toward the old ravine where it seeped down into the sandy ground and passed by and through the cadavers. Then it hit the clay sill and followed it until the bluff where the water trickled and puddled and seeped down the hillside next to the stairway.

V

1982. From 1869 to 1982 the quarantine station master's house several times underwent re-roofing, re-wiring, and re-plumbing. Even the floor joist undersills, infested with powderpost beetles, had been replaced. Years ago the vault-like brick cistern fell into disuse and over time it, too, was lost to a covering of new soil.

In 1982 the old house sheltered a family of three: Joseph Storey, a local person who grew up to work at the pulp mill; his wife, Sandy, who, raised in Port Angeles, never wanted to leave the Olympic Peninsula; and their project-preoccupied son, Michael, ten. Sandy stayed home and kept one eye on the small business files in her at-home accounting business. The other eye she focused on her son. Among his activities, the boy was a gardener. For several years he had arranged lawn space for his own gardening. Rows of onions, carrots, and lettuce pushed up against a line of blueberry bushes in his well-weeded patch. On the other side of the blueberries, rhubarb plants presented bright red stalks that held elephant-ear-sized green leaves. Michael shared his crops with his parents, but most of it he sold within the neighborhood. His prices could not be beat. Ten cents for three stalks of rhubarb, a nickel for ten strawberries, five onions for a quarter, each carrot, a nickel. A pint of blueberries sold quickly for thirty cents. With his earnings he paid for his own baseball mitt and for some of his wet suit gear. Last fall Sandy stopped with Michael at the University of Washington in Seattle, and at the herb garden she pinched Welsh onion and giant fennel seeds, all of which now stoutly grew in Michael's garden.

Often, when their son was not in their presence, the parents discussed what topics to talk about when conversing with Michael.

Their goal was to teach him mathematics, geometry, physics, and music without his knowing he was the subject of a learning effort. For example, as part of their desire to influence their son to appreciate the outdoors, they spent over a thousand dollars to buy wet suits and snorkeling gear for all three. Together, on weekends, they'd go camp at a river. During the time there they would change out of their clothing, put on swim suits and then put on wet suits. At the river's edge their face masks would be pulled down, the breathing tube would be inserted and then they would float, face down, with the river. Below, bright and odd-shaped rocks came into view. Trout flitted by. Long strands of freshwater seaweed bent with the current. At some places of bottom mud they could see the tops of fresh-water clams. In the Hoko River they could expect to see three-foot-long black eels. In the Duckabush River they knew they could float down and salmon coming upstream to spawn would swim right toward their face masks and then veer off. On the Soleduck River they floated, looking below for black, red-spotted, stones of orbicular jasper. Later, at home, Joseph took a sledge hammer to each of the collected rocks to reduce their size so that they would fit into the rock tumbler. Michael sold the finished, polished rocks to a downtown tourist store for twenty cents each.

Last summer and then the present summer, the family had developed a new river project. They looked for places to leap from ledges into the river. In late summer the rivers on the west side of the Olympic Peninsula warmed, so a wet suit was not needed. But on the east side, the two rivers with the best jumps, the Dosewallips and the Duckabush, remained frigid. From suggestions from Quilcene friends they learned that at the top of the Big Quilcene River canyon, just below an initial grotto, was a twenty foot waterfall that could be reached by roping down the steep hillside. The river fell into a pool that was thirty feet deep and it was possible to jump from the ledge, swim back and to easily climb up the rocks right to the ledge.

Another place they went was four miles up the Duckabush Valley Road where there stood some picnic tables and ample parking space and a trail that ran south and, along the way, was crossed with logs that once served as skids when oxen pulled segments of downed old growth trees. The trail led down to a place called the Ranger Hole where once there was a waterfall that later was dynamited by the government in the hope of allowing salmon to swim further up river. Here, ledge leaping became a favorite activity for the Storey family. Before jumping they tied a rock to the end of a long line and tossed it where they intended to jump to learn if any logs were stuck deep down in the dark water. Directly below the ledge was a backwash, but three feet out the river ran fast. The trick was to jump far out and to land in the main river. The jumper would disappear underwater, and then the buoyancy of the wet suit would pop the swimmer to the surface. Then the river would quickly carry him about forty feet down stream where he could swim north into the eddy. The eddy would carry him ashore where a path led back to the ledge.

The last time Joseph, Sandy, and Michael jumped at the Ranger Hole, they went at night. Except where their flashlights beamed, it was pitch dark. The walk through the forest had been quiet. Once at the jump ledge, the river sounded loud and busy, in a hurry to get somewhere. As each jumped, all the other two could see was the dropping light. It then disappeared beneath the water and for seconds the light was dispersed underwater, like a light at the bottom of a swimming pool. Then the light moved in the rapid current, became carried by the eddy and slowly moved in that backwash up stream to the walkout point.

SCUBA lessons were planned. Money had been reserved for the cost of the lessons and for more gear. But it never came to pass.

VI

"Son, you ready?"

"No, never, this wet suit is too small. It's like an unfriendly rubber band," replied Michael.

Michael and his father, each in a wet suit and wearing swim fins, walked backwards from the parked car at the northwest corner of Fort Worden State Park toward North Beach. They continued backwards across the beach to the water and waded in. Cold water seeped inside the wet suits.

"Yikes!" exclaimed Michael, "this is cold, torture!" Each knew that body heat would warm the water that had leaked inside the wet suits and that thereafter they could swim farther out without being chilled. Millions of microscopic air bubbles within the neoprene wet suit would insulate the swimmers.

When water depth allowed swimming, they pulled on glass-faced diving masks and snorkels. Each, leaning forward, swam into deeper water. It was nighttime. Neither had yet turned on his waterproof flashlight. Phosphorescent microbes flashed, glowed, and disappeared.

When they switched on their flashlights, a new world appeared: colorful rocks; sand moving with the swells; iridescent flags of seaweed; bullhead fish sprinting, settling, then sprinting again; shrimp daintily walking, looking for food. Father and son, floating, slowly kicked their swim fins and proceeded into deeper water. Soon, below, fields of shiny green eelgrass came in sight. Hundreds of stems and blades, four feet long, bent and undulated with the tidal shore current. The eelgrass served as food for migrating brant geese. When covered by the tide the eelgrass rose as a protective area for small marine life. Herring eggs could be seen, as though glued to the blades of grass. The direction of the tide changed four times a day, and with each change the eelgrass would be pushed and brushed to the new course. That night the surface of the water had no whitecaps, no ripples. It lay calm except for a gentle swell.

In one of the open sandy areas between stands of eelgrass, Michael saw two eyes looking up. He tucked and made a shallow surface dive to get a better look, and as he approached, the body below the two eyes shook and tremored, sending up a small cloud of sand. The flatfish emerged from its hiding place and swam away. That fish had been born with its eyes on opposite sides of its head, but as it matured, one eye had slowly migrated until both eyes were on the same side. This enabled it to lie perfectly flat on, and sometimes part way underneath, the sand.

In another sand patch a huge Dungeness crab felt threatened by sounds and lights above. It did not run for shelter. Instead, it settled down on the back edge of its carapace and raised its claws, wide open, straight up, ready to pinch anything that came within reach. Joseph flashed his light ahead. The light beam ran into dark stems and fronds of a kelp forest in deeper water where the sand beds changed to cobble stones and boulders. At full growth the kelp might be as long as thirty feet. Air captured inside the stem and bulb of the kelp provided floatation. Sometimes the kelp became so buoyant that the kelp would float away, lifting a cobble stone, to which it was anchored, with it. In that way, cobble-stones, over thousands of years, moved around the beaches of the Pacific Northwest.

Michael shined his light toward the nearing kelp bed. Iridescent colors reflected off the long blades of fronds that extended from the kelp bulbs. The light stopped as it shone into a forest of black kelp stems, for there, close to the swimmers, was a stem that hosted a large spider crab. Its skinny long legs somehow allowed purchase on the stem. The crab made no move as the swimmer passed.

Their destination was an erratic, which is the name given to mammoth rocks pushed and carried by glaciers thousands of years ago. The glacier would advance hundreds of miles, pushing, smothering, crushing and rounding the edges of such rocks—and then the glacier melted away, abandoning its contents. Granite formations do not exist on the Olympic Peninsula, but in fields and forests near Port Townsend there lie exposed many granite erratic boulders. The one toward which Joseph and Michael swam was exceptionally large, about twenty feet in diameter. It rested on a clay sill like a cue ball might rest on the green felt of a pool table.

Now, as they swam, the water was about fifteen feet deep. When Michael flashed his light down, he no longer saw eelgrass. A brown stubby algae plant covered much of the bottom. He noticed black lines moving below him and realized he was looking down on the backs of a school of perch. Ahead, about six feet below the surface, black objects appeared stationary in the water, but as the swimmers came closer the objects turned and as a group disappeared into the kelp. Just before the fish disappeared Michael recognized them as a school of black bass. Joseph and Michael moved through a school of candlefish and the silver sides of the fish reflected back the beams of light. Thousands of them, moving in unison, skitted away from the swimmers.

The underwater flashlights picked up a black wall ahead. The wall, which was the side of the erratic boulder, lost its blackness as the swimmers neared, and it became the source of varied forms of sealife. Bits of colorful seaweed anchored to it. Clinging purple sea urchins stood out. Bright orange starfish slowly moved on the rock. Flowerlike white sea anemones held on. Some had necks three inches thick that extended from the rock a foot and a half and then produced a billowing whiteness like a white peony. Small fish accidentally swimming into that whiteness would be paralyzed by toxic substances. The sea anemone would close over the fish and pull it down inside its neck, where the fish would be consumed.

Michael's light settled on a patch of what appeared to be carnation flowers. He knew what he saw was a cluster of piling worms. He reached forward and touched one "flower," and instantly it contracted and disappeared down its leathery tube. Over the rock, hundreds of pairs of gem-like bright spots reflected back. His light was entering the eyes of shrimp and then reflecting back off their retinas. At one place on the rock large barnacles were fastened to it. Michael swam close and could see into their open bodies. Periodically, from each barnacle, a hand-like stalk would emerge and sweep through the water, seeking to net whatever food might be floating or swimming by. Then the mouth stalk would disappear back into the barnacle, to re-emerge seconds later.

The top of the rocks rested about a foot below the surface of the water. Swells, obstructed by the rock, rose up and gently washed over it. Michael and his father swam to the rock top; then each rolled over, and they sat there with their snorkels and face masks removed. The swells pushed at them but lacked enough volume to sweep them off the rock. The darkness around them was broken by the revolving light at Point Wilson. For sixteen seconds a white light shone their way, lighting up the tops of the half-submerged bulbs of kelp, then fading. In one second a red light shone for just one more second. Then there was a brief moment of darkness and the rotating white light repeated its cycle.

"Dad, what was that humming sound in the water? You hear it?"

He replied: "Look over toward Whidbey Island, see that patch of brightness? See how it is slowly moving north?"

"Yes."

"Looks to me like one of the cruise ships running out of Seattle, going to Alaska, and what we heard was its engine sounds coming through the water. At least, that's my guess."

"Could it have been the sounds of a nuclear sub?" asked Michael.

"Probably not; they're designed to run quiet."

They sat there and talked for a while. Slowly the slight exchange of cold water into the inner side of their wet suit chilled them and they left the rock and swam to shore. As they walked along the beach back to shore, different shore birds moved out of their way. They heard the protesting sounds of a tern, then, a short distance later the chatter of two leaving oyster-catchers. Just before the parking lot they came upon a great blue heron that had been hunting in the shallows for minnows and shrimp. As it flew away, it uttered guttural reproaches.

Back at their home, after washing themselves and their gear with fresh water, they sat at the kitchen table telling Sandy of their adventure.

VII

"Where's Michael?" Joseph inquired, coming in from his shift at the pulp mill. His wife appeared from the kitchen, kissed him, and replied, "Walkabout—he's on one of his beach trips looking for salvage. How's the mill?"

"OK. I think I'll take a shower. Mill is fine. Starting a new product, making heavy kraft paper coffins for crematories in India and Pakistan. Big market potential."

After the shower he and his wife sat in the dining room and drank coffee and chatted. He fingered a cookie, knowing it was not good for him.

"Why does Michael do that beach patrol?" Joseph referred to the habit his son had of waiting until just after a major storm swept Port Townsend. Then the youngster would leave the house and follow the beach from the lagoon to Point Hudson and, sometimes, on to Point Wilson, looking for anything of value that might have blown onto shore. If the tide were high when he walked by Chetzemoka Park, he'd walk right through the salt water.

She smiled. "Why not? Being young is learning to do your own thing, however unexpected. He gets exercise. He stays interested in life. And once in a while something valuable does float in, like the leather jacket that we rinsed in fresh water and that he sold for $30."

"I guess you are right. I mean, people in places like Ireland would check the shoreline for shipwrecks, and then the whole community would salvage whatever was tossed up on the beach."

In the room where they sat there was not much to suggest how old the house actually was. The ceiling was unusually high, eleven feet. Dented wainscoting ran along the length of one wall.

Above the electrical light hanging from the middle of the room was a simple circular plaster of Paris medallion, two feet in diameter, secured to the ceiling when the house was built.

Often Michael would find big pieces of lumber and lug them home, piece by piece. When the pile began to be an eyesore, he'd draw up a rough list of the types and lengths of wood and submit the itemization to a neighbor, who did building construction and would offer two or three dollars for the latest pile.

A door opened and in walked Michael carrying something heavy in a sack.

"What's in the bag?" asked Sandy.

"Dead bird."

The parents looked at each other and rolled their eyes.

"Can we look?"

"Sure."

Michael opened the sack and his dad peered in.

"That's a loon. Where'd you find it?"

"Blown in on Fort Worden beach."

Sandy looked in the bag and said, "Can you see? The eyes, the bird's eyes are still red. It has not been dead very long."

Bothered, his mother tried not to look, and asked, "What are you going to do?"

"I want the skull and the beak. If I bury the whole bird at the bottom of the compost pile, in a year or so, only the bones will remain and then I can bleach the bones to clean and to whiten them."

There could have been a big argument, a row starting with an exclamation like, "You fool, taking a protected animal from a state park. Get that bird out of this house!" As it was, the parents pretended nothing unusual had happened, and their son left to bury the loon.

A week later a storm approached from the north and brought rain. Conditions worsened and the beach cliffs near Port Townsend turned muddy. Moisture seeped down the cliffs. The water pried open cracks along the cliffs and loosened pieces of bluff fell down to the beach. While walking logs along the beach near McCurdy Point, Michael Storey glanced at the bluff wall and noticed a serrated bone.

"That's a tooth, a mammoth tooth," exclaimed his father when Michael lugged it home. "A fossil like that has value." Sandy phoned around and learned where Michael could sell the petrified tooth for $100.

A month later the parents took $200 from their own savings to buy their son a metal detector. Michael had read about gold. He learned in school that the bluffs consisted of rocks, sand that, just like the erratic boulder, had been pushed and carried hundreds of miles out of the north by glaciers. He reasoned that the ice movement must have scraped up some gold nuggets and pushed those along, too. His thought was that as the bluffs eroded, the gold nuggets would fall away and accumulate amongst the other rocks on the beach. The tooth had come from the north, so why not gold, too? Although he did search, the only gold he found was jewelry put by accident in garbage and tossed off the community bluff near Cape George.

On some weekends the family would drive to Glenn Cove to capture crabs. They would float over the muddy clam beds, out to eelgrass where the Dungeness crabs walked along the bottom. When they saw one, Joseph would surface-dive down and would reach behind the crab to grab it. Back at the surface, the crab would be placed in a large catch-bag held by Michael. Both of them had to be careful not to brush up against the bag. Back at the house, Sandy would have a large pot of boiling water ready to cook the crabs.

After awhile, in addition to walking beaches, Michael took to swimming in his wet suit just off downtown Port Townsend. He quickly learned that petina-green colored metal objects sticking from the bottom were pieces of copper and of brass that often had value. The bottom was covered with pieces of old boats, sailors' garbage tossed years ago from rowboats, and collapsed wharves. Off Tyler Street he found the outline of a ship that had burned there at low tide—and only oak ribs and the lower hull remained. It was his secret that the spots of green in the oak marked where brass dowels remained. Each dowel was three-fourths of an inch in diameter and twenty inches in length. The challenge was to extract the valuable rods.

One weekend at tea with her husband she told him of her concern that their son had such a fixation on accumulating money. "Look how he is stretching himself, walking beaches, wet suiting, selling vegetables, just to make more money. Where's he get his energy?"

She talked on for a while and then Joseph said, "Well, I do not know why he goes after money so much, but maybe it is because we do. You do accounting for others and I spend eight hours a day to make brown paper. Maybe he is in his own way mimicking us. Where is he now?"

"He's out back, making a lemonade stand. He took the old bathroom door that lay in storage, now, for a table, and he's going to rest it on two sawhorses. I told him he could have an old blanket as a cover for the lemonade table."

"That professional look," commented Joseph.

"Yes, that professional look." And they laughed.

Joseph asked, "Should we be out there helping him?"

Sandy answered, "Beats me. He seems happy. He can ask for help if he wants it."

"He sure is determined to earn money. That last lumber pile went for $12.00. Where is the lemonade stand going?"

Sandy answered, "He says he is setting it up at the foot of the concrete steps, just at the foot of the stairway. He said he plans to be open on Sundays to catch the church crowd. Do you mind?"

"No, it's fine with me."

VIII

The next Sunday, Michael lugged his gear down the concrete steps and set up his lemonade stand well before church let out. A hand-painted sign declared "FRESH LEMONADE—30 cents." No one going to church bought, but afterward, out of thirst or charity, they nearly bought him out. The lemonade remaining on hand was only enough for a cup and a half. Two teenage boys walked his way. Michael wanted to sell two cups, so he poured from his pitcher one full cup and then filled a second cup halfway. He took the half-full cup, walked back by the concrete steps, and let the trickling seepage fill it. He had no awareness that the water in the cup had passed by the cadavers placed there many years ago.

"Hey! Last two cups. Reduced price. Want some lemonade?" They ignored him.

"Hey! Big price reduction here. Last two cups. How about a dime each?"

As they walked by they still paid no attention to Michael.

"OK! You win! Closeout sale. Lemonade for you at a nickel for a cup. How about it?"

At that the teenagers stopped and passed a dime to Michael. Michael watched to see if the one drinking the thinned drink would notice. Nothing said. No refund demanded. The two boys gulped their drinks and set the cups back on Michael's table. Michael commenced to take his stand apart, to store until next Sunday. He glanced down to the far corner of the block where the two boys were walking. To his amazement he saw the teenager that had drunk the adulterated lemonade haul off and hit the other, knocking him down. Then the attacker jumped up and down, stomping on his companion.

The following Sunday, the sun warmed Port Townsend. No shore wind cooled the place. After church, lemonade sales were brisk. Once again Michael had a cup and a half of lemonade left and again he topped off the last cup by resorting to the water that dripped and seeped down along the concrete stairway. Along came the town banker, a big fat man chomping on a cigar, and his petite, quiet wife. She was so skinny she looked as if she had never eaten a meal. On her head rested a small pillbox hat that appeared to be held in place by a long hatpin. He was so rotund, that his belly fell forward and down over his belt. He looked as if he had never in his life missed a meal.

"Maude, you want a drink? Some lemonade?" He really wanted something for himself. Out of politeness he pretended to want to meet her needs. She nodded affirmatively.

"Two drinks, young man!"

He put down sixty cents.

Michael passed the full cup of lemonade to the banker. Then he gave the banker's wife the cup that was watered down. He looked out of the corner of his eye to see if she would notice that the drink was half-strength. She said nothing and when she had emptied her cup she put it down on the table and walked away with her spouse. Michael made himself busy removing the stand, but he kept watching the banker and his wife as they walked on. When they were about four houses away, Michael saw the wife reach up and pull out the long hatpin. The banker was looking straight ahead. She reached up and placed the point of the hatpin just outside her husband's ear. Then with the open palm of her free hand she hit the end of the hatpin and drove it into the man's head.

No one suspected the thinned lemonade as a cause for violence, except Michael, who said nothing. As things developed, there would never be another Sunday lemonade stand. One day during the week Michael's parents loaded their car with debris to take to the dump. Though the Jefferson County Commissioners had been warned that the Jacob-Miller Road turnoff to the dump was just in front of a blind curve, the commissioners ignored the opportunity to correct the hazard. As Michael's parents slowed and then began to turn left, an oncoming car, speeding, came into sight too late. It hit the Storeys' car just behind the right front tire, lifting the vehicle off the ground and spinning it a full circle. By the time it came down it was a ball of fire. No one in the accident lived.

Relatives from Maine flew out and took Michael to a new home. Over the many years that followed, Port Townsend became for him a memory of loving parents and of life near the sea.

IX

Richardson Bones, FBI Director, chaired the emergency meeting. In attendance were the Vice President of the United States, the Joint Chiefs of Staff and the head of the Centers for Disease Control. Very restless, Bones glanced at his watch, reading the time, 2:36 P.M., and the date, Friday, June 12, 2008.

Bones' eyes hurt from inner pressure. His doctors reported he had glaucoma and most likely would become blind. He could not concentrate on the subject of the meeting. His thoughts were on retreating to the balcony adjoining his office to lessen the pain by smoking another marijuana cigarette. His last joint was an hour ago and his breath still smelled of marijuana. Bones could tell from the frown on the forehead of the Vice President, a self-righteous born-again Christian, that his marijuana breath had been detected. The Vice President was looking coldly at others, wondering who was breaking the law.

Bones tried to move things along. "Gentlemen, thanks for being here. This is mostly a meeting about a medical matter. Maybe Dr. Gerry Kravic, from the CDC, could explain. Dr. Kravic."

"Thank you. I was asked to be here by Director Bones to share with you information about a smallpox vaccination. As you know, there is some concern that the smallpox virus may be in the control of one or more terrorist groups and might be used against United States troops and civilians. We do not at this time have a vaccine to immunize large numbers of people against such terrorist activity. The papers distributed to you contain letters from a Mr. George Willets of Seattle. He has been sending the CDC and his Congressional Delegation pretty much the same letter for the last six years. Basically, what he says is that he happened to be reading at random different books in the library stacks at the University of Washington and he came across three books that described in three separate geographical areas the same technique for making a smallpox vaccine right on the spot, so to speak—no pun intended—but to make a vaccine just as a smallpox outbreak began. By his thinking, if there were a smallpox attack, say, in Paris, it would be possible to go there and to remove the fluid from the swellings of smallpox victims, especially those who appear only modestly sick, and to use that fluid as a vaccine. One book cited by Mr. Willets describes how the Chinese would let the fluid dry, grind it into a powder, and then, for a vaccine, would inhale the powder. This meeting is to determine to what extent, if any, our military forces and civilian defense groups should give credence to the information in the endless letters from Mr. Willets. Some Congress people are asking me why Mr. Willets' letters have so far been ignored."

The real reason for the meeting was that everyone knew the Vice President and the President were so religious that they did not believe in vaccinations. Rather, they relied on the righteous actions of God. Because the President was also Commander in Chief of the US armed forces, he could order no research be done with regard to defensive vaccinations. Bones had been pressed by Kravic to somehow get around the White House so the military could study what Mr. Willets disclosed—and in response Bones had called today's meeting.

Bones glanced up, this time at a wall clock, hoping time would go by. His eyes glanced for a moment at a glass case next to the clock. In it hung the dress, slightly stained, once worn by a lady who had had an affair with a former president. Bones looked at the others in the room. The Vice President appeared to be not paying much attention to Dr. Kravik. He looked like he was on the verge of asking who in the room had been smoking pot. The two women and the one man that formed the Joint Chiefs of Staff listened intently. They knew the history of smallpox and appreciated any information as to how to blunt a re-emergence of the disease.

"Director?" a voice called to him from behind his chair.

"Yes, Pauline, what?"

His secretary leaned forward and passed him a note:

"Director, I know you wanted all incoming calls blocked, but something unusual has happened. Three times someone from Colorado has phoned for you. Each time I can barely understand what he is saying because he is crying. He says you owe him a favor from something he did for you in the sixth grade. He says his name is Benny. He is on hold right now, sobbing and crying on the other end."

"Benny?" wondered the Director. "Benny!" His mind moved away from the Vice President, who, having cut off Kravic, was speaking of God's will as more important than human planning. Bones forgot about the pressure on his eyes. He remembered the favor. Winter. Snow. Ice. He had been walking his brown Labrador along Frenchman Creek just south of Haxtun. The dog had gone off on its own and had walked onto thin ice over the river. When the dog fell through, Richardson was too scared to go out on the weak ice to save his dog. Each time the dog tried to climb out, the ice broke. Pretty soon the cold weakened the dog until it paddled just enough to keep its head above the water. Along came Benny, a classmate, who immediately lay down on the ice and snaked his body toward the dog. The ice made some cracking sounds, but it held. Benny reached far ahead, grabbed the dog's collar, and pulled the dog his way. The weight of the dog kept breaking the ice, but Benny moved backwards, away from the new edge, still holding the dog. Within a few feet the ice was thicker. Benny pulled the dog up onto the ice and told it to lie still. Then he moved backward, pulling the patient dog until they reached shallow water, where it did not matter if the ice held. Richardson, grateful to have his dog back, had thanked his classmate and had said, "Benny, I owe you one."

"Yikes," thought Richardson. "He helped me. I never did anything for him."

"Mr. Vice President, ladies and gentlemen, please excuse me. I have received a message that necessitates my attention. Please just go on" ("with your nonsense, Mr. Vice President," he thought.) "I will be back in a few minutes." The Vice President was clearly annoyed to be interrupted and to have the Director of the FBI leave the room while he was talking, but there was nothing he could do.

Outside the meeting room Bones told his secretary he would take the call on the phone extension on the balcony. That way he could smoke a joint while talking.

"Hello, Richardson Bones here. Benny?" All he heard was someone crying. "Benny? Hello?"

Then he heard a faint "Yes."

"What is up? Why are you calling? Why are you crying?"

"My son, Tom, has disappeared. Just gone."

"He moved away?" asked Richardson.

"No, disappeared."

"Tell me what happened."

"He had been living with us, helping us run the farm south of Haxtun. Nine days ago he drove over to Sterling to buy food for us and he never came home. We called the sheriff at midnight, and a deputy spotted the car in the grocery store parking lot at Sterling. The groceries he bought were in his car. Sheriff suggests he was kidnapped. We can't run this farm without him. He had a good job teaching social studies at the Haxtun High School. The sheriff says he hasn't a clue as to what happened." Then Benny started crying again.

"Benny? Listen to me," said Bones. "OK? I owe you a favor for saving my dog. Here is what I will do. At this point the FBI lacks jurisdiction to help. Regardless, the FBI Denver office will be instructed by me to send someone to meet you tomorrow. That agent will also check with the Philips County sheriff. A report will then be sent to my office and I'll get back to you. I am sorry about your son. Take care. I have to go back to a meeting. I am going to turn you over to my secretary and she will ask you some questions, like where you now live. Let's hope your son shows up."

"Thanks."

Six days later a file came in from Denver:

"To FBI Director Richardson Bones. Per your instructions, Agent Smithal Thomas on Saturday, June 13, drove to the farm of Benny and Gudrun Edwards located a few miles south of Haxtun, Colorado. He spoke with them for about an hour and then he met with the local sheriff, who showed him the impounded car of the missing person, Tom Edwards. The facts appear to be that the son is truly missing with no explanation and no clues. The sheriff believes Tom Edwards was kidnapped. Await further instructions."

After Bones read the report he phoned the Edwards farm.

"Benny? This is Richardson. A report has come in about your son that more or less repeats what the sheriff said. I have no idea what happened. I wish I could bring your son back to you. I am sorry about what you and your wife are now going through. If I can do anything more to help you I will, but for right now, until further facts come forth, all I can do is instruct the Denver office to meet with you and your wife at your home at least once every six months for the next two years. I'm sorry I can not do more."

Benny thanked him and they rung off.

X

July 20, 2008. The passenger bus had left Chicago hours before. On stretches of Interstate 90, the driver conversed by CB radio with truckers ahead to learn where the state troopers were not. He would increase the bus's speed up to ninety-five miles per hour until the truckers reported a speed trap when he would reduce his speed to sixty-five miles per hour. The roof of the bus was rigged with an illegal radar detector, which also helped the driver detect a trooper ahead and slow down in time. On its westward course, the bus sped over Iowa in full light. By the time the west boundary of South Dakota was crossed, the sun was well down. In darkness the bus began to cross Wyoming. Most of the passengers leaned back and tossed about, trying to sleep in seats seemingly designed to deny rest. Above the driver a sign read: "DO NOT TALK TO DRIVER WHEN BUS IS IN MOTION."

From the back of the bus a passenger rose and walked forward.

"Excuse me, could I ask you a question?"

"Certainly," replied the driver.

"Most of the time since Chicago we have been moving at a fast clip, but now it seems to me you are driving slower and I wondered why? There is hardly any traffic on the interstate and it is a divided highway. Why don't you go faster?"

The driver did not directly answer the question. Instead he asked the passenger to simply look for a few minutes at the road way ahead of the bus. The passenger did and commented that he saw nothing to answer his question.

"See that?" the driver asked.

"No, what?"

"Wait, there will be more."

Two miles later there was a big reddish splotch on the cement, and it looked as though something had been dragged off the road.

"There, recognize that?"

"It looks like blood," answered the passenger. "Roadkill?"

"Yes, that is why I am driving slower. This is open country and antelope and deer jump the fences along the interstate and are hit."

Just then the bus headlights picked up frantic movements ahead and the bus braked down to twenty miles per hour.

"Darn!" muttered the bus driver. He and the passenger saw a line of antelope moving at a full run onto the highway, off the highway, and then back onto the roadway. The lead animal was a female antelope trying to wean her near-adult young. Her only hope was to outrun them, and she was mindless of any traffic on I-90.

For a second, as the bus pulled alongside the animals, it looked as though the bus would be able to pass, but the mother turned and dashed directly in front of the bus.

KWHHAAM! Most passengers slept through the sound of the impact. Upon impact one headlight went out. The windshield was covered with blood, short hair, and fecal material. The driver turned on the windshield spray, activated the wipers. The dark blood turned to a thin pink and then disappeared. The driver turned to the passenger and said, "Now, does that answer your question?"

Around midnight a lady came forward to chat. For the driver, it broke the monotony of driving. She described her neck operation and then asked the driver if he had any hobbies.

"Mostly just one, making artificial lures for fly fishing. I have a work table at home, many types of hairs to use, like polar bear hair, mountain goat hair, and an assortment of bird feathers." She was not interested in fishing and returned to her seat.

The bus pulled on through the night, leaving Wyoming and entering Montana. At 3:00 A.M. a passenger came forward and explained he had to urinate, and the on-board bathroom had been occupied by the same person for the last thirty minutes. The bus driver had no desire to demand entry to the bathroom, so he told the passenger to just wait a few minutes until the bus reached a pull-out.

"When we get there, we'll stop. Just walk off the road a bit and take a whiz. Maybe some other passengers would like to shake a leg. Please don't walk too far, for sometimes the sagebrush is thick with ticks."

Shortly, the bus slowed down. It moved across the fog line into an informal rest area. Some trash barrels were there, but nothing else. The door opened and the passenger walked away. Most passengers remained half asleep, tortured with discomfort in the bus seats. Even with one headlight, the area ahead, to the side of the road, was almost as bright as day. The driver glanced back and saw that the bathroom was still occupied. He stepped off the bus and walked alongside it. Overhead, the stars of the big sky country speckled brightness. The driver looked for the Big Dipper and then used it to find the North Star. Clumps of sagebrush stood near him. He walked back toward the front of the bus, glancing at the trash barrels and at the empty beer cans and plastic bottles that had not quite made it to the barrels. Pieces of blown truck tires lay about. Between two sagebrush plants about twenty feet away from the bus, he saw what appeared to be a patch of antelope hair. "An addition to my collection of hairs for tying flies," he speculated. He walked over, reached down, grabbed the hair, and pulled. Nothing moved. He tightened his grasp and pulled a second time. Up rose the hair. Attached to it was a human head with most of its skin.

XI

August 10, 2008. George Herrington lived like so many men: earning money in order to pay child support to his former wife. His marriage had collapsed three years before. Sending child support payments each month and arranging child visitation were his only residual contacts with his spouse. He did not earn enough money to invest or to marry someone else. Anticipating visitations with his eight-year-old son kept him going. His divorce papers decreed when he could pick up his son for the weekend visitation, and he knew he had to drive around for another ten minutes before he would have his son for Friday night, Saturday, and Sunday until 5:30 in the afternoon. As he walked towards his former home, the front door opened a crack, then wider, and out darted his son Bruce.

"Pops! Hi."

"Bruce! Good to see you. How's Bruce?"

"Fine. Where we going this weekend?"

"Well, weather looks good. Yellowstone be OK?"

"Sure."

"Jump in and off we'll go."

Once again, for the duration of the two days, a weak semblance of family structure was restored to George Herrington.

From Bruce's home in Livingston, Montana, they drove south down into Paradise Valley, by Emigrant, through Gardiner, and camped at Mammoth Hotsprings five miles into the park. Cost ten dollars to camp there, and the sites were illogically crammed right next to the roadway. As service trucks made loud noises going up and down the steep hill next to the park, it became difficult to sleep. Elk nearby bugled, and the way they sounded it was as

though each was announcing a serious health problem. Twice during the night, what sounded like hundreds of coyotes yapping and
howling at the same time were heard by George and Bruce. In
the morning they climbed out of their sleeping bags just at
dawn.

"Put on two extra wool sweaters, and grab a towel," suggested
George. The rest of the campground appeared lifeless. No one else
was up. They walked to the northeast corner of the campground
and then followed a trail that went downhill to the Gardiner River.

"Should we keep a lookout for grizzly bears?" asked his son.

"Yes, but it must be rare to have bears around such a busy place."

Along the river they reached a cave from which a smaller river
emerged. The water of the smaller river was hot, varying between
116 and 130 degrees Fahrenheit at different times of the year.
Then it flowed about 150 feet and cascaded into the chilly waters
of the Gardiner River. Locals knew that at certain times of the year,
when the Gardiner was not flowing too fast, people could move
rocks around within the water and create a protected pool in which
to sit and relax in the confluence of the two rivers. The park keeps
quiet about the hotspot. The maps disclose nothing.

"Should we go nude?" Bruce asked.

"No, keep your undershorts on, for a ranger could appear when
you least expect and then we'd have to leave and we'd get hit with
a fine." They left most of their clothing on the river bank and
slowly waded into a makeshift pool where the Boiling River, steam-
ing and hot, dropped into the Gardiner. Some pockets of water
were simply too hot to enter. At other places the hot and the cold
water had mixed and it was possible to hold on to bottom rocks
while the heated Gardiner swept by. A year ago, Bruce and George
had been at the same place with a metal detector to see if they
might find any gold bracelets or wristwatches that others had lost
to the swirling pressure of the river. They found nothing.

Later in the morning they paid to stay a second night, and
then drove north to Chico to see if they could find the trail up

Emigrant Mountain. There, they did find a small parking lot and a single trail leading off toward the mountain.

"Want to walk the trail for a bit?" George asked.

"Sure."

Fairly soon the valley spread out before them. Spots of cows could be seen and sometimes heard. On the far side of the valley was a strip of highway running between Livingston and Yellowstone. Sagebrush once covered the valley floor. Big houses on five-acre parcels now dotted the landscape. Pretty soon there'd be no valley range left for cows, let along elk, antelope, and deer.

"Bears, here, too?" asked Bruce.

"Yes, but not likely. Look around. All this tumble of rock, a scree, does not offer much food for a bear. A tree might fall and termites or ants might take up lodging, but even though bears eat them, it is not much of a full meal, for the bugs are so small. Besides, except for a few trees, this is mostly open country. If there were a bear ahead we'd probably see it. The bear would see us. Chances are we'd then go in opposite directions."

Before it got too dark they returned to the campground and walked down once more to the hotspot. They sat in the hot water just before dark, then got out, dried themselves, put on dry clothing, and walked along the Gardiner River. Bats flitted overhead. Upon seeing a herd of elk along the trail ahead of them, the father and son turned back and returned by another way to their campsite. In the evening they placed on the park picnic table a board that had ten holes spaced across the top. In each hole a candle was placed and then lit to provide light while they played backgammon. In the morning they planned to look for gold.

Early the next day, gear packed, they cleared out of the campgrounds. They drove north to Emigrant and turned east, and after crossing a bridge over the Yellowstone River they turned right and drove down into a public area for fishermen to park after sliding their riverboats off trailers into the river.

"Here is our plan," explained George. "Our gold detectors can be used underwater. Put on your wet suit and I will put on mine.

THE WHARF AT PORT TOWNSEND BAY

We will leave the car here. You and I will simply wade into the river and float down three miles to the next public access area. Then we will get out and hitch-hike back. But you must promise to refrain from telling your mom we hitch-hiked. OK?"

"Fine. Do you think we will find gold nuggets on the river bottom?"

George knew they would not. Any gold would be 19 times heavier than water and would have moved down below other bottom rocks to the bedrock. But he wanted to maintain a sense of hope in his son. He answered, "I am not certain. They do call the river 'Yellowstone' which suggests gold."

"I mean," continued Bruce, "has anyone else done this?"

"Not as far as I know. No one has our sense of imagination."

Privately, George did wonder if they might drown or become impaled on a sharp piece of metal sticking up from some car junked in the river. He said nothing.

One might argue, and surely his former wife would, that the father was deceiving his son and exposing him to unreasonable hazard. From prior river floats, both George and Bruce knew they would see fish, bright rocks, and unexpectables as they floated along, peering down into the river through their face masks. To each of them it was exciting. They were ready.

"Remember, son, if you see a gold nugget or if your metal detector goes 'YYYEEEEOOOOUUUUUUUHHHHHH!!!!!!' and if the river is flowing too deep to allow you to stop, then grab the plastic sack tucked around your belt. Pull the end that contains the rock and let it fall to the bottom as a marker. The rock will sink fast and will hold the plastic sack in place, like a flag on the bottom. We can come back in a boat and find the sack and then look for the gold."

"What?" replied Bruce. "I can't hear you. My wet suit hood is on." George removed his thick, black glove and poked a finger under Bruce's neoprene helmet to expose his ear and repeated what he had just said.

They walked to the river edge, turned on the metal detectors, and waded out into the flow. Water pushed against the left side of their legs. Deeper they walked. Once the face masks and snorkels were in place, they each bent out forward and floated on the river. They swam to the middle to avoid downed trees, sweepers, along the banks.

Their float had commenced. Quickly, the river carried the father and the son under the Emigrant bridge. A person on the bridge, looking down, and seeing the face-down, lifeless forms, would think they had drowned, unless the observer noticed the snorkel breathing tubes sticking into the air. No guide. No boat. Just a father and a son floating on the Yellowstone, having the adventure of a lifetime. With the spring snow melt over, the river ran fairly low and slow. The water was clear. What they observed below appeared like an endless sunlit scroll of rocks, boulders, bullhead fish and other fish, and trash. Each let his metal detector hang down a few feet, closer to the bottom. Every five seconds the metal detectors each emitted a "beep" sound. "Beep" then a five second pause. "Beep" then a five second pause. Some rocks looked bland, but others had quartz crystals and fool's gold crystals that stood out brightly and reflected the sunlight. The detectors were set to only sound an alarm if gold were encountered, not pretty rocks. All they heard the first two miles was the infrequent "beep." George floated right over a water-logged tree. Part of a branch extended up close to the surface and it ripped into his wet suit, lacerating the skin on his chest. For a moment he was held there by the tree. The current had carried Bruce farther down the river before George could extricate himself. Once free he started swimming down the river to catch up with his son. "I'm bleeding. My ex would say I deserve this!" he surmised. He swam the Australian crawl stroke, head down, breathing through the snorkel, slowly gaining on his son. He was tired. His chest hurt. His peripheral vision noticed something white ahead on the bottom. He was going to float right over it when he realized it was his son's white plastic sack. "Must have worked loose," he guessed. Just then his

metal detector increased its beeping and went into a
"YYYYYEEEEEEAAAAAAAOOOOOOLLLLL!!!" of a howl.

"Gold? Gold!"

His son had removed his face mask and snorkel tube and had
rolled over on his back and was yelling "GOLD!" repeatedly to his
dad. George pointed toward the shoreline to direct Bruce to leave
the river. They caught up with each other at a grove of cottonwood
trees lining the river bank.

"Let's walk up river and maybe we can see the plastic sack
from the shoreline."

Up river about three hundred feet Bruce exclaimed, "There!"
Sure enough, flagging about on the river bottom, George could
see a smudge of white.

"Look, Bruce, you stand here. I will walk further up and swim
down to see what may be there. We may have to make several
passes." He did not tell his son he was bleeding. "I'll use you,
standing here on the water's edge, as a reference point to help
locate the sack."

A few minutes later, he re-entered the water and swam out to
where he thought he might float over the sack. Then he raised his
head and waited until he saw Bruce on the bank. Then he looked
into the water for the sack and saw it about forty feet ahead. Whatever Bruce came across had to be upriver from the flag. George
drew a deep breath and then he surface-dove down to brush along
the bottom. All he saw were rocks and boulders. The sack was
coming closer into view. Suddenly, when he was certain he was out
of air and had to surface, he noticed below him a muddy mound
with a chain wrapped around it. The end of the chain was about
three feet down river from the mound. He was passing fast. He
grabbed the chain and his hands slipped to the chain's end. The
momentum of his body going down the river and suddenly being
stopped by grasping the chain caused the chain to tighten, but
the mound did not budge. His body twirled around by the force
of the river until his head was upstream. Just the tip of his snorkel
broke the surface of the water, enough for George to breathe. What-

ever was in that muddy mound, all that gold, did not move. George rested, letting the river flow by him as he held on to the end of the chain. He noticed some blood joining the river where it had come from the cut on his chest and had oozed out of the rip in his wet suit.

Breathing extra air, he pulled himself down the chain until he gained against the river's pressure and achieved footing. Then he pulled up on the chain with all his strength. The river helped, for as it pushed against him the pressure transferred to the chain and then down to the mound. At first nothing happened. Then the mound started to move. A cloud of mud and silt blocked George from seeing the chained object rise from the river floor, but he quickly perceived he was floating down the Yellowstone River with a chain wrapped around his arms and a bundle hanging below.

Reaching shore just as his son caught up with him, they carried the bundle up the river bank to a clearing.

"Dad, what is it? Would a nugget of gold be wrapped in black plastic?"

"Bruce, I have no idea. Please give me your Swiss pocket knife. I'll cut through the plastic and then we'll see what's there."

"Dad, wait. Don't do anything yet. Let's turn the metal detector back on and see what it does." When the metal detector "on" switch was turned it began a rapid beeping sound, and when the detector was moved next to the bundle, it started a screaming yowl.

George removed his gloves. Even though his fingernails were soggy and weak he managed to unfold the blade. As the knife cut through the plastic it stopped upon something hard. "I'll cut a square, a window, so we can look in." When he did he saw bones.

"Bones! Probably an illegally killed deer."

"A wealthy deer," remarked Bruce.

The other end of the wrapping had a bowling-ball-sized roundness. George cut there. First a wall of bone appeared and next to it was a hole, an eye socket. Next to that was another hole with pieces of dangling nose cartilage. Below that was what remained of a human mouth. The teeth were lined with gleaming gold fillings.

"Wow," exclaimed Bruce. "Look, there is a crawdad crawling out of the right eye. Can I have the skull for my special shelf at home?"

George was wondering how this all would be explained to his ex-wife. He could just imagine his uptight, freaked out former wife now seeking a court order to cut off all child visitation.

"Well," he answered, acting as casually as he could, "that might be really nice; soak it in the kitchen sink for a couple weeks, study it later for a couple months by placing it in the big aquarium tank that stands just inside the living room front window, then letting it dry on the porch before placing it on that special shelf above your bed. Yes, that might be just the ticket. But, Bruce, I am afraid it is the law that when anyone comes across a dead body the sheriff has to be alerted, and ten times out of ten, the deputies will take the body to learn how the person passed away."

"Can I at least write my name and phone number on the skull so the deputies can send it to me later?"

George could just see his former spouse opening the mail.

"No, I think not. Let's figure how to get out of here with our new cargo. Not only do we have to float down the river a bit more, but we have to swim to the other side."

XII

August 25, 2008. In an upper bleacher at the stadium in Sioux City, Iowa, Lynn Field watched the high school basketball playoffs. Mostly, she stared at one player, Ron Bog, for whom, since observing him in their organic chemistry class last semester, she had a crush. He had the nicest, cushiest-looking lips. Her goal was to figure out a way to kiss him.

First, she approached her father and asked if she might borrow the family speedboat, a restored 1936 mahogany-planked thirty-one-foot craft. At the stern was a cockpit for two; then the varnished deck advanced forward to the engine hatches. It kept going forward in flashy long lines of mahogany planks to the chrome fixture at the bow, which contained the red and green running lights for night use. Permission was granted, on the condition she operate the boat north of the I-90 bridge crossing the Missouri. Then she got up her nerve. After the Hindi class Lynn approached Ron and asked if she could take him out for dinner and for a boat ride the next Friday. If he were going with anyone, she knew he'd refuse to go out with her. A pleasant surprise, he accepted.

That Friday her dad gave her the ignition keys and cautioned her: "Lynn, please be careful on the water. Keep your speed down and watch out for careless boaters. Some drunks out there. Not too much to worry about. Stay out of the way of tugs and barges. One reason for keeping your speed down is that if you do hit a partially submerged log, the damage to the hull will not be too bad—and you and your friend will not get bounced out into the water. Also, please keep an eye out near the shoreline for solitary swimmers." She thanked him for the keys. "There's plenty of fuel. Just in case there might be gasoline fumes in the engine compartment, be sure and run the ventilator fans for about five minutes before starting the motor."

The dinner went fine. Lynn and Ron practiced speaking Hindi. After she paid for the meals, she drove Ron to the marina. She pointed out the speedboat and together they unsnapped and removed the canvas tarp covering the cockpit.

"Have to run these fans for five minutes," she remarked. "Then we can take off and go up river and water ski."

When she turned the ignition the engine roared, "VVVRRRRUUUUMMMMM!!!!." As the engine heated the exhaust changed from a thick black plume to a clear transparency. "OK, just leave the ropes on the catwalk. We're off."

The boat growled its way through the marina and out onto the Missouri. When about 500 feet from shore, the sound of the motor changed to a deep-throated scream as Lynn advanced the throttle. The intake carburetor, its valve fully opened, guzzled gas. The bow rose upwards and the stern hunkered down. Then as the boat began to plane, the bow lowered and the stern rose to skim and bounce along the surface at 48 miles per hour. Several miles upriver, Lynn stopped the boat. Upon opening the engine hatches she reached down and pulled out of a side compartment a pair of water skis, a towing rope, and a portable ladder. Ron skied for a while. After Lynn explained how to run the boat and watched him operate the craft from a starting position to 20 knots and then back to being stopped, she took her turn at water-skiing. Later, when the skis and rope had been tucked away, she kept in place the ship's ladder. She and Ron dove off the boat and used the ladder to get back on board. It was getting dark. She produced some beer. Ron declined. They floated downriver and just chatted. Lynn kept an eye for the running lights of other vessels. She thought it more romantic to be in darkness, so she did not turn on the speedboat running lights. The evening lights of Sioux City glimmered on the east shoreline. To the south they could see the traffic moving on the I-90 bridge. The smooth water reflected the more distant lights from the westerly Nebraska side of the river.

They took turns singing songs and telling stories. Ron revealed he had an excellent memory for reciting poetry.

Hoping to get closer to Ron, Lynn said, "I think I'd like to dive into the dark water. How about you, Ron?" .

"Sure."

She dove and then he followed. Underwater it was pitch black. Her plan was to remain in the water longer and to pretend to be weak so he would help her up the ladder. That way he would be holding on to her and perhaps close enough for a kiss. The boat was floating closer to the bridge. After Ron climbed out, Lynn waited a few minutes and then made her move. She swam to the edge of the boat and asked for help in getting out. He leaned down, grabbed her hands and helped her up the ladder. She sort of fell on him, as though by accident. She made no effort to remove herself and simply remained half on him and half off. "This is comfy, Ron," she cooed. By this time the boat was almost directly under the bridge. Ron took the hint. He turned his face toward her and his lips moved toward her expectant, pursed lips. Just then: "SSSSSLAAAPPPPP-WWWHHHAAAAAMMMM!!" Something slippery, putrid, and fleshy was all over them and the dashboard.

Her plans were ruined. The boat reeked. They reeked. Lynn swore a streak. The basketball star looked up at the bridge, as they passed under, and remarked: "Do you suppose anything else is going to be tossed off? Look, something just splashed in the river! There, further west, something else! Somebody is driving west slowly and tossing things off the bridge."

Lynn was crying. "What are we to do? How can I clean my parents' boat? They will be so disappointed in me. Let's move this mess into the river."

"No, Lynn, it is illegal to toss waste off the bridge. Place what we can on the forward deck where it won't go anywhere. We can clean ourselves easily by jumping overboard. Back at the dock, with a little cleanser and some bleach, we'll clean the boat, good as new. I'll use the phone at the marina to call my cousin. He is a deputy sheriff."

XIII

September 8, 2008. Two guards at the Hanford Nuclear Facility in Eastern Washington left a cloud of dust as they made the seventh perimeter drive. Sometimes a rabbit ran across the gravel road. Coyote spotting was not too infrequent. A rattlesnake slithering on the roadway served as a diversion from a boring job—and the driver would veer the truck over the snake. That part of the Columbia River did roll on. There, for about fifty miles, the river remained as one of the few areas in Washington State where it was not bottled and stilled by hydroelectric dams. The guards, armed, were on the lookout for intruders. In their own minds, though unspoken, each was also on guard for his own personal safety if the underground tanks of highly radioactive fluids should overheat and explode. When the pickup truck reached the northeast corner of the facility, the driver said, "Look, there's my brother."

The other guard looked around and saw no one and said so.

"Saddle Mountains! Look upriver and just above the Saddle Mountains."

"OK, but I see nothing."

"Well, I see him. He flies his hang glider there. See that little dot in the sky, just to the right of the transmission tower?"

The other guard took out his binoculars, leaned out the truck window, and looked: "Yes, I see him. From this distance he looks to me to be floating in one place, but now I see him turning. I didn't know you had a brother."

"He keeps to himself. As a kid he was talkative, and we did a lot of things together. But after being drafted years ago he served in Vietnam in the mortician division—and he went quiet after that. His wife runs a cafe in Othello. Their home is right next to

Crab Creek, near Smyrna, and they have a natural cave on the acreage—way back in the cave the entire passageway becomes blocked with ice, that, according to him, formed thousands of years ago."

"Isn't he a bit old to be hang gliding?"

"Well, he's been doing it almost daily for many years. He's on disability. More bird than human, he knows what he's doing. Maybe, I can reach him."

The driver reached for his cellular phone.

"Charles! Henry here. Can you hear me?"

The two men waited and then they heard "Affirmative."

"I am down at Hanford and can see you way up there. How are you?"

"Fine. Yourself?"

"OK. How's your family?"

"Fine. Yours?"

"OK. Take care," said the driver.

"You, too."

The guard started the truck and turned to his co-worker. "See that. My brother doesn't say much."

Earlier that day, Charles Lea had left his home at Smyrna and had driven through cool desert air to the top of the Saddle Mountain ridgeline south of Crab Creek. Tightened bungee cords held aluminum tubes, dacron cloth, and nylon ropes to the top of his old car. The air remained cold as he removed gear and assembled his hang glider. Slowly, a tumble of fabric became stretched and curved, forming in about 45 minutes an aircraft, a hang glider, strong enough to carry Charles. He knew the air remained too cold to do anything. He had to wait for the sun to rise higher. Then the sun heated the desert below which, in turn, heated the air. Some of that heated air would become pressed together, forming a large pocket of air much warmer than the air nearby. The heated air, a thermal, weighed less than the cooler air, so as the force of gravity pulled downward, the cooler air went downward, squeezing the thermal upward, out of the way. To pass time, Charles hiked down the north slope of the Saddle Mountains. He'd walked there many times before and knew where to look for pieces of petrified rocks. The surface rocks remained cool, so he thought it remained too cold for the scorpions to be up and about. He glanced at a cliff below him. It had a vertical face impossible to descend. He traversed the hillside, dropped down around the cliff to its foot, and then scrambled horizontally just below the cliff. Along the cliff face he saw numerous round holes in the lava rock. He'd seen lava tubes before. He looked closely in one dark hole and inside he saw a whitish circle with bright eyes in the middle staring and blinking back at him. "Barn owl," he thought. Another hole looked like a ravens' nest. On the way back up to his car he came across a heavy piece of smooth, opalized petrified palm tree.

He was still early. The sun began to heat the ground. After entering his car he turned on NPR and lay down in the back to listen to the radio in the event he did not doze off. An hour later, the heat of the day had commenced. The car's interior was baking Charles. He stepped out and prepared to cool off by taking flight.

When he gripped his hang glider, the heated aluminum spars felt too hot to touch. He buckled his belt to the glider and then raised it over his head and walked toward the edge of the mountain. Faster he went, until running, he ran off the ridge. For a few feet the hang glider decreased elevation as though to crash, but then the increased air flow provided lift. Within seconds he was 100 feet from his car, then 300, then half a mile, soaring over a thin thread of Crab Creek directly below. Now he had to find a thermal to lift him. Without that hot air he would simply glide about, downward, until he landed below. Then he would hike up the mountain and drive down for his gear and start all over.

He saw a hawk soaring, about three-fourths of a mile away. He steered toward the bird and watched it. Sure enough, the hawk's elevation changed. It moved upward, even though its wings remained locked in an outward position. Charles continued gliding toward the hawk. By the time he reached it he had lost 200 feet and the hawk soared in a big circle way above him. He felt the air on his skin warm and the glider banked upward ever so slightly, telling Charles he was within a column of rising hot air. He turned and banked again and again to remain within the lifting air. Up and up he went, the hawk still above him. Finally, the hawk dropped away. Charles rode the hot air up to 10,000 feet. At that height the Columbia River looked like a narrow rope, and Crab Creek appeared lost in crowding sand dunes.

The day was getting on. Charles knew there would be many thermals. He shifted his body weight forward to place the hang glider into a descending glide and from two miles up he soared downward, over Beverly, out over the Columbia, and banked slowly over Wannapum Dam. Eight thousand feet lower he found another thermal and rode it up to nine thousand feet. He looked west. Snow and glacier-covered Mt. Rainier shouldered up above the rest of the Cascade Range. As he turned the glider he saw the I-90 bridge at Vantage. Trucks crossing there looked to Charles like spots of dust moving in a line. Just north of Vantage he could see the cliff that rose from the river and the many layers of lava, each of which had in times long past flowed red hot in molten liquid across the terrain. As the glider kept turning he glanced down at little lakes of blue, the potholes, collecting drainage through the sand from Moses Lake, which he could see further on. On one descent he soared down and glided along the ridgeline of the Saddle Mountains, only fifty feet above the passing sagebrush and exposed rocks. Then he banked over the emptiness and, finding another thermal, regained elevation.

He heard the birds before he saw them. A flock of several hundred geese, its "V" formation constantly losing and then regaining its form, flew south along the Columbia several thousand feet below him.

He looked at his wristwatch and saw that the afternoon was about over. In a while the thermals would be gone. Charles decided to call it a day. He put his glider into a gentle glide toward his car. When he was 500 feet above his vehicle he noticed circling black spots just beyond Crab Creek. Out of curiosity he banked sharply and swept out away from the Saddle Mountains to get a closer look. "Vultures," he commented to himself. He saw jet black bodies, black wings, and small pink heads. He glanced to the ground thinking he'd see a dead cow or horse. Nothing was in sight, except a thin track on the ground from the nearby asphalt road. The track was visible as it covered a sand dune for several hundred feet and then it stopped. He knew the path could only have been recently formed, for the frequent winds would move the sand about and cover any track. Curiosity got the better of him; he decided to see what attracted the vultures. Once he landed he could look about, and then he'd leave the hang glider there and hike up to his car. In a broad circle his glider descended down over the slope of the mountain. Boulders and rocks and occasional sagebrush quickly passed below. Ledges and cliffs were of no consequence to him. Shortly, he flew below the vultures. Gently, Charles settled into a slow glide that was just a few feet above the sand. When he shifted his weight astern, the craft responded by stalling, lowering him in a standing position onto the sand. One moment he had been airborne, now he ran a few steps and then stopped with graceful fabric wings overhead held up by his arms. After unbuckling and setting the hang glider to rest on the sand, he walked toward the path.

When he intersected the trail in the sand he quickly realized it was made by human steps. "Someone walked here and then returned to the road, probably to bury the family dog," he speculated to himself. Upon walking the route of the footprints to their end, he saw that the sand there was disturbed. Kneeling down, he dug into the sand with his hands. The sand at the surface was hot from the sun's energy, but further down the sand felt cool and still moist from a heavy rain two weeks ago. Sure enough, someone had dug a hole and then filled it in. Three feet down his hand ran across smooth plastic. He scooped more sand and saw a black surface. "This is sure stupid," he uttered. "Nothing here but trouble. No treasure. Bad news. Just bad news."

Below him he saw a heavy-gauge black plastic sack wrapped

with a cheap laundry-line rope. He dug around the sides of the
sack. Finally, with his kneeling body braced by one hand against
the sand, he reached down and pulled at the cord. The sack lifted
a few inches and sand sifted down into the new void, so each time
he stopped lifting, the sack rested at a higher level. When the sack
was clear of the hole, he took his knife and cut away the rope.
Overhead, the vultures circled closer. He placed the sack on its
end and opened the top. At first all he saw was darkness. Then he
saw the outline of an arm. Reaching gingerly into the sack he
pulled out a muscular arm. A wristwatch was still there and he
compared it to his—it was on time. A gold-plated cufflink held
together a long-sleeved formal shirt that still covered the limb.
Charles Lea reached in again and pulled out a knee joint attached
to a lower leg. The foot remained covered with a polished leather
shoe. Coming up from the shoe, around the leg circled a blood-
splattered white sock. Not much scared Charles. He lowered his
hand into the sack again and pulled out something roundish with
a visible mess of bone and flesh. A head. He turned the bloody
stump in order to look directly at the front of the head—and there
he saw the face of a handsome young man.

Quickly, he refilled the sack, dug out the sand that had fallen
into the hole and then placed the sack in the hole and covered it.
He took off one of his socks, tied it to the fallen branch of sagebrush, and jammed the branch in the sand as a marker above the
body.

He pushed buttons on his cellular phone. Maybe his brother
would still be at work.

"Hello?"

"Clarence, that you?"

"Yes. That you Charles?"

"Yes."

"Why are you calling?"

"I'm up Crab Creek from Beverly about two miles."

"OK, did you crash?"

"No, Clarence, I came across a body of a young man. His

limbs were cut away. Looks like he was recently murdered. Could you put in a call for the sheriff?"

Clarence knew his brother never joked. "Yes, I will do that right now. Goodby."

Clarence's earlier phone call from Hanford to his brother had been intercepted and recorded by the FBI security there. For a while an FBI agent had used a telescope to observe Charles Lea fly from thermal to thermal. Then the FBI picked up Charles' call to Clarence.

As he was about to push a button to disconnect his cellular phone, to his astonishment, Charles heard:

"INTERCEPT! INTERCEPT! THIS IS AN FBI INTERCEPT! DO NOT DISCONNECT. STAY ON OPEN LINE."

"What?" answered Charles.

"This is FBI Agent Marc Collins at Richland. We want that body. Do not move it. Do not leave. We know where you are and a military helicopter will be there in twenty minutes."

The agent reached over and pushed several buttons. The engine of a hidden Apache attack helicopter coughed into operation and the concrete bunker roof overhead began to roll back. Alarms sounded there and at FBI headquarters and at the airbase at Oak Harbor. The blades increased in RPM, and just when the roof had pulled back, the helicopter quickly rose 100 feet and then dipped in the direction of the security building. At the building roof the helicopter touched down and reduced blade RPM enough for Agent Collins to climb on board. Then the helicopter rose 200 feet, dipped to the northeast, and at max speed moved across Hanford to the Columbia and then it flew up the reach to Beverly and took a steep banking turn east to follow Crab Creek.

Charles could hear the sound of the approaching helicopter. He had heard many in Vietnam. Strange, he thought; before he had listened to the same sound and knew bodies were being brought in to him. Today, it was the reverse. He had a body and the helicopter would take it away. The helicopter pilot had no trouble spotting the hang glider. It hovered 400 feet overhead and then moved several hundred feet north in order to land on the asphalt road.

Together the agent and Charles dug out the plastic sack. The agent made one quick look inside to make certain that there really was a body. As the agent wrote down a quick statement, they could hear sirens growing louder. Soon, three deputy sheriff and two state trooper cars were parked near the helicopter. Even though the officers left their vehicles, they kept on the overhead red, blue, white, and yellow flashing lights. The officers taped off the area and then mixed plaster of Paris in the hope of getting car tread imprints and shoe prints, but the soft formless sand did not offer any reward. They placed the body in the helicopter. When the agent realized that Charles' car was up on the mountaintop, he offered him a ride. In a few minutes they lifted off, and as the helicopter ascended the darkening slopes, the agent explained that a bulletin had recently issued from FBI headquarters to be on the lookout for discarded remains, especially of young men. "After we drop you off we will land at the Tri-City Airport and transfer the body to an FBI Lear jet that will speed it over to the FBI forensics laboratory in Seattle. Have to be careful, for there might be incriminating fingerprints." Charles stood by his car and watched the helicopter disappear down the Columbia Reach. The sun had fallen below the Cascades, leaving a fading sunset of an afterglow of apricot gold. He walked to the ridge and looked down. The flashing lights of the vehicles sharply punctuated the advancing darkness. He realized how easy it would be when he drove down, with all those flashing lights there, to locate his hang glider.

XIV

On September 20, 2008, Bones signed the following letter:

From: Richardson Bones
        Director, FBI

To: Benny Edwards
     P.O. Box 24
     Haxtun, Colorado 80731

Dear Benny,

      Reports have come in describing the unexplained disappearance of young men in other states. Somehow, I think there is a connection between each event. The FBI is assuming jurisdiction over these cases, including the disappearance of your son, Tom.

      Hopefully we can find some explanation for what has happened. I will write to you as soon as I learn more.

                              Richardson

    Two days later members of a new FBI team were called to the Director's office for their first meeting. Toward the end of the gathering, Director Bones said, "I'd like to thank you all for attending. As you may know I am on the edge of going blind due to glaucoma. By my doctor's directions I must leave now to go smoke a joint. Because some of you arrived after the meeting commenced,

I am asking my assistant, Agent Michael Storey, to come forward and give you all a summary of what this meeting is about."

Michael rose from his chair and walked forward. He waited until the Director exited the room and then he turned to the fourteen men and women in the room.

"You each pretty much know why you are here. Four days ago I e-mailed to each of you the details. Some of you may wonder why the FBI is involved, for no single incident describes a matter clearly within FBI jurisdiction. The truth is that the young man missing from northeast Colorado has, or had, a father who was a grade school classmate of Director Bones. We are on the case with or without jurisdiction."

The people listening knew that Michael had a history of not talking much. But they knew that what they heard would be right to the point.

"Our goal, through your help, is to find an explanation as to why in the last few months single young men have disappeared. We suspect that similar disappearances have been going on for about five years and have only now come to our attention. In some of the recent cases, human remains have been recovered. Your papers give you the details. It appears young men are kidnapped, killed, and their remains are discarded farther west. Only legs, arms, and heads have been recovered, except for one incident where the intestinal tract was tossed off a bridge over the Missouri and landed on the occupants of a speedboat. For some reason the trunk or body of each victim is being retained by the killer or killers. The dismembered limbs have been studied at the forensics lab, and the lab reported that at each place where a leg or an arm was cut away from the victim's body, a device like a shear was used. In each case, it was the same shear. Lab photographs show the cutting edge of the shear to be uneven, and when used, it left a pattern of groove lines across the surface of the bones."

An FBI agent put her hand up and on being recognized asked: "Shear? What do you mean? Can you describe it better?"

"Thank you," Michael replied. "Let's see how I can do this.

Sometimes when there is a serious auto accident the occupants are trapped inside. In most cases the emergency response team will then use a device, called the Jaws of Life, which is more or less a very large and leveraged pair of metal snips, to cut away the car metal and free the passengers. That device is a shear. In our situation someone used shears to snip off human limbs.

"We believe at least eight men are missing. Parts of four have been recovered. The remains of two were identified by parents. DNA analysis confirmed another. The fourth remains unknown. We do not know who is doing the killing. There is considerable worry that with the recent number of disappearances that the killings will actually increase. Your job is to stop the killings by finding the killers."

Michael glanced at his notes. "I've said just about enough. The papers you have show the clues known to date. Briefly I'll recap that for you.

"Clue Number One suggests some sort of ritual. Of the four men whose body parts were recovered, dismemberment was exactly the same: arms cut off just above the elbow; legs cut off right above the knee; and lastly, ghastly, each head was sheared free just below the thyroid.

"The second clue comes from the first, for it is clear from the lab report that no saw, ax, or knife was used to do the cutting. Instead, a powerful shear, as I mentioned, appears to have done the snipping. Possibly, the biggest clue is that the shear's cutting edge left a signature of lines and grooves on each bone. That suggests the killers used the same instrument in all the killings.

"A third clue remains mostly a puzzle. It is the similarity in age and sex of the deceased. The ones we know about were single and between twenty and thirty years of age."

Another agent raised his hand and asked, "Do the missing people have anything in common, like membership in the same church or club?"

"I am coming to that. Each of the eight reported missing persons worked as a school teacher. One was a music teacher. One served as a Spanish instructor. Two coached football. Another taught chemistry. One taught English part of the time and apprenticed as a school administrator the rest of the day. Another taught French and also did work of the school janitor. The eighth person ran a vocational shop class. There was one class that each taught as an extra load to his regular schedule and that was a class dealing with social studies."

An agent asked "Social Studies? That's very general. What did teaching Social Studies involve?"

"As far as I can tell, it looks like the instructors developed a student consciousness of social values to prepare the kids for their own future. Sounds vague, I know, so how else can I tell you? Well, each led student discussions about dating, study habits, getting along with family members, saving money, and whatever the students wished to be considered."

Another agent asked, "Did the teachers know each other?"

"That is presently unknown."

Someone asked, "Is this one person?"

"No, it appears there are at least two. When body parts were thrown off the bridge the vehicle on the bridge kept moving, suggesting one person drove and at least one other did the tossing.

"Well, this meeting is over. Your individual assignments are in the papers provided to you. Time is important. Good luck."

As the agents began to leave, one that knew Michael Storey walked over and conversed with him. Upon learning that Michael was about to leave for a month's vacation he asked where.

"Not too sure. I may visit a town where I once lived as a child and where my parents are buried. I have never been back."

XV

October 5, 2008. The harbor at Friendship, Maine, opens directly toward the Atlantic. Storm winds push lines of white-cap-topped waves down Muscongus Bay right smack into the harbor, jostling the lobster boats and breaking up on the mica-spotted granite inner shoreline. Back and forth across the harbor tacked a seventeen-foot Friendship catboat. Its gaff-rigged mainsail could not hold the beam gusts and again and again the old hull heeled over, allowing saltwater to almost pour into the cockpit. At the last moment Shelly Muir let out the main sheet, and the sail spilled its wind and the mast returned to a near vertical position. Shelly and Jake Lawrence enjoyed storm sailing. Doused with spray and bothered by the knocking about of the hull, they assessed each breaking wave and each gust of wind as to what its destructive capacity might be. On that day they assessed each other, too, for Shelly wanted Jake to agree to marry. Jake wished to comply but believed his parents needed his time.

"Look, Jake, you decide: me or your parents. We have dated for three years. I'm ready to settle down, to have kids."

Jake said nothing. He looked at the next wave. Its foaming length approached the port beam, reached under the boat and lifted it. The hull sprang up and the mast tilted downwind. Shelly let out a little on the main sheet.

She was persistent. "Jake, I need you to tell me now. Are you going to live with me or are you staying with your parents?"

He never said a word. She presented him with an impossible situation, for he loved all three. Later, Shelly tacked the craft to just downwind of its mooring buoy and then she turned upwind. Jake, at the bow, reached forward and secured a mooring line to the buoy. A long tether line ran from the buoy to a rowboat. After pulling up the centerboard, placing the rudder within the cockpit, and furling the sail, they used the rowboat to reach shore.

Shelly knew Jake's silence was his "no" to marriage. His parents had won. Just before they parted she remarked, "OK, we are done. Just remember, your parents will not live forever, and then who will you have?"

"Thanks for the sail," he said before closing his car door.

At Waldoboro, from the street, he could see in through the kitchen window. His mom was leaning over the sink. He knew she was struggling to breathe, a victim of emphysema from years of smoking. She could walk about six steps before she had to stop and breathe for a few minutes. Her lungs were shot. On entering the house he greeted her, and she warmly responded. "Oh, hi Jake, good to see you. Been sailing with Shelly?"

"Yes, good wind. When's the last time you went out on the water?"

"Oh, Jake, years back. Your dad had a chum who owned a Friendship sloop, and we'd sail on it. One time we went out as far as Monhegan."

"That is a long one."

"Yes. Speaking of your father, he is in watching TV."

Jake walked into the living room and sat near his dad. The old man's face had been blankly staring at the TV. As he realized his son was there, a smile formed on his lips and he turned away from the TV. "Well, look who's here," he said. "How's things?"

"Just fine," Jake lied. "You?"

"Just fine," his father lied.

Jake knew that his dad's operation for artificial knees had not gone well. He also was aware that his dad had constant pain from spinal column stenosis.

Most nights Jake's mom went to bed early. Jake stayed up as long as his father. Many nights Jake's father prepared for bed and took his sleeping pill, then became curious about what might be on the television set. He'd forget about going to bed. As he watched, his medicine took effect, causing the old man to be so unsteady that only when Jake was there to shoulder him could he reach his bed with the assurance of not falling down.

"Say, Dad, you going to be in your chair for a while? I'd like to skip over to the store to buy some eggs."

"Sure."

"I'll be back in about forty minutes and then I can give you some arm support when you decide to go to bed. OK?"

"Thanks, son, appreciate your help. Which store you going to?"

"Over toward Wiscasset."

Inside the store at Wiscasset, Jake had no awareness of being followed. Two half-gallons of two percent milk, a dozen eggs, two loaves of six-grain wheat bread, and a magazine for his mother cost $9.20. Upon reaching his car he opened the driver's door and leaned way in to set the sack of groceries on the floor in front of the passenger seat. He stood for a second, ready to move behind the steering wheel. He felt a hard object press against his ribs.

"This is a gun," he heard, "do not move or you will be shot."

Caught totally unprepared, Jake had not the slightest idea how to respond.

"What is this? Who are you? What do you want?"

"Close your door and walk with us to the back of the black van."

He complied. They made him enter the back of the van and then they locked it and drove away.

In the front of the van, Vern Mapledork and his wife, Donna, congratulated each other on their capture. They drove inland. On the Interstate heading for Boston, Donna turned to Vern and said, "Now?"

"Yes," he replied. She reached down to a floor lever and turned it. Smiling, she remarked, "Goodby Jake!"

Just as the re-directed exhaust entered the back of the van they could hear Jake pounding on the walls. "Won't last long," commented Vern. His left hand held the steering wheel. The right hand rested on Donna's left thigh. In a few minutes the pounding stopped. Donna and Vern were so elated with their murder, they pulled into the next rest area and held each other and necked for half an hour. Then they drove to an isolated place within that rest area and opened the back door enough to allow fresh air in. Within a few minutes they entered. Jake had no pulse. He was gone. His parents would never see him again. "OK, let's go to work."

From an overhead rack they lowered a huge pair of leveraged shears. "Snip" went Jake's left arm. "Snip" went the right. The shears were then positioned above the left knee. "Snip" went the lower leg. In a moment the remaining lower leg was dismembered. When the shears were placed below Jake's thyroid there was a crunching, snapping sound before the head fell free and rolled on the van floor. While Vern cut into the stomach wall and began to remove the organs, Donna triple-wrapped each limb and the head separately in black plastic. She waited until there were no other vehicles at the rest area and then lugged each wrapped piece and placed it in a dumpster that stood nearby. After she disposed of the sack containing the entrails, she removed garbage from a second dumpster and dropped it over the plastic bundles.

A refrigerated compartment in the back of the van had been designed to hold the torso. From opposite ends of the compartment, Donna and Vern lifted the lid and rested it to one side. They rolled and twisted the remains of Jake's body to the edge of the compartment and pushed it over the edge. It thudded to the compartment floor. Once the lid fell in place, Vern set the thermostat for 36 degrees Fahrenheit. Still making sure no other cars had stopped at the rest area, Donna turned on an electric pump that drew water from a holding tank and forced it through a hose that she used to cleanse the back interior of the van. Within minutes the van returned to the Interstate. In a few hours, near Boston, it would turn right onto I-90 for the long haul to the West.

Three days later, as the van crossed through Spokane on I-90, Vern radioed ahead. "Van to Base. Van to Base. Do you read me?"

A female voice responded: "Base to van. Please state location."
"On I-90 passing through Spokane."
"Was your trip successful?"
"Yes."
"Very well. Congratulations. Please proceed to Port Angeles."

They traded off driving. When Donna drove, Vern slept in the passenger seat. When he drove, she found she could not get comfortable, so they stopped to allow her to enter the back of the van. There she slept soundly on the lid above Jake. It took seven hours to reach Mercer Island and an hour and a half to get through Seattle's traffic congestion to the ferry at Edmonds. The ferry run lasted 25 minutes. Two hours later, the van pulled into the parking lot behind the Clallam County Courthouse. In a few minutes a heavy-set couple, dressed well, left the courthouse building and walked toward the van. Courtesies and keys were exchanged. The van's motor started and in just a few minutes the van proceeded further west along Washington State Highway 101. Vern and Donna had been directed to another car and they knew it was for them to use to drive home.

When the van reached Lake Crescent, it was driven to a secluded shoreline campground. There, several couples sat around a campfire. They were waiting for the van and for darkness. When it was dark, one couple left the group and walked down the dirt road a distance—just to be on the lookout for park rangers. Another couple walked to a nearby dock and started up the outboard on a small runabout. In a few minutes the runabout came out of darkness and edged up onto the shoreline close to the van. Its running lights remained off. Then two couples pulled Jake upwards and out of the van and placed his body within a white box. All the couples there then grabbed part of the box and helped carry it to the boat, where it rested mid-ship, from gunnel to gunnel across the hull.

The married couple on the boat, Rance and Shirley Smacks, let the others push the boat away from shore. They lowered the motor and started out onto the lake. Shirley stayed at the wheel and Rance took a compass bearing. Then he turned on the depth finder. When the depth finder showed that 970 feet of water lay below, they slowly lined up the boat with shorelights.

"OK," Rance said. "We are positioned. Let's do the drop." They pushed and pulled at the coffin box until it was balanced on one gunnel. The boat tipped to one side due to the off-center weight. Then the box slid into the water. It floated next to the boat. Shirley handed Rance two thirty-pound sacks of sand. He reached over and tied each sack to handles at one end of the coffin. Holes in the coffin allowed water to enter and soon the box was mostly submerged. "One more sack, please," he commented. Shirley passed it. Just as he tied it the box began to slip down under the water.

"Is he going to be right side up or upside down?" asked Shirley.

Rance replied, "Honey, I'm sorry I did not notice. Our work is done. Let's go."

She asked: "What do you suppose it looks like down there? I mean, it is dark, but if one had a light down there I wonder what would be seen."

Rance thought for a moment. "Remember the stone monuments on Easter Island—how they sort of stand upright with no buildings or other structures around?"

"Yes."

"Well, that might be how the bottom would appear, for we have sunk so many boxes containing bodies that the bottom must look like Easter Island, but instead of stone faces, here there are white coffin boxes standing on the weighted end in bottom mud."

"Maybe," Shirley said, "the bottom scene might appear as though someone had set out commercial bee hives at the wrong place; white boxes standing about and no bees."

XVI

October 7, 2008. Port Townsend, Washington. There the grave-stone lay: "JOSEPH MAURICE STOREY and SANDY STOREY." Along one side of the stone he placed a vase of bright yellow roses and on the other side he put down a vase of red roses. Michael had no idea if his parents were in one casket or, if in two, whether they were alongside each other or one above the other. He read the letters sandblasted into the granite. The dates of birth varied, but the time of death was the same: August 16, 1982. His memory of his parents was enhanced by the two photographs he had kept of them in his wallets over the years. He knew he had been loved and appreciated. It was his parents, he knew, who had made him appreciate and to feel comfortable being outdoors, like camping for extended periods of time. His most central thought was one he wanted to crush, namely, that a stairwell would form in the grass and both his parents would walk the passageway to simply greet him, talk with him, and to start again with him as a renewed family. The deepening sadness he experienced was interrupted by the ringing of his cellular phone.

"Michael? Is that you?"

"Yes."

"Richardson Bones here. What are you doing?"

"Standing next to the gravesite of my parents."

"Michael, look, sorry to catch you this way, but I want you to know that two days ago there was another disappearance."

"Another young man?"

"Yes, at Wiscasset, Maine. Car left in supermarket parking lot. Groceries in car. No signs of struggle. No surveillance cameras. No clues. Parents were dependent on son and now he's gone. Tragic mess. When are you returning to work?"

"Well, Director, I just got here. I'd like a little time to re-visit the place where I lived as a child. I have not been here since 1982."

"OK, OK, sorry to cut in on you, but I need you back in my office to help solve this case. Can you shorten your vacation?"

"Maybe, sir, but I just arrived. Give me some time. If I can return early I will. With no clues, there is not much to do except to send out all-points alert—suggesting an upgrade of police patrols of grocery store parking lots. The ongoing lab work may come up with something, but I'm not part of that anyway."

"All right, Michael, just get back here as soon as you can."

Michael walked between many gravestones on his way across the grass to his rental car. Some gravesites had clumps of iris. An unopened beer can leaned against one stone. Near the car a madrona tree stood. Its branches hosted waxy green leaves and a flock of noisy crows. The tree had no bark, its trunk and branches formed a smooth surface that mimicked human skin. Before getting into his car he glanced down into the valley. He could see Port Townsend Bay, the Jefferson County Courthouse, and farther to the left, the high school. He stared at the school, realizing he would have graduated there if only the county commissioners had cared enough to abate the hazard at the turn-off to the county dump.

The route from the cemetery to his motel did not take long. Down Discovery Road to the golf course, then along its line of poplar trees on "F" Street to where it changed to Tyler Street, then left down Lawrence Street, to Monroe. From there, right down the hill near Point Hudson to Water Street. Then right through the historic downtown area to a huge sign that said "Bay Motel." He turned left there, parked, and went in to register.

"Preference for a room?" the clerk asked. She looked like she was still in junior high school. Maybe her parents owned the motel.

"Well, yes, I'd like a top floor towards the outer end, please."

"Room 9323. Here's your key. It has a balcony with a hot tub and is on a corner, so you can see most of the downtown and the outer bay."

"Thanks. I noticed in your brochure that you have rowboats and wet suits available for guests?"

"Yes, this motel is fairly new. It's built over the beach out into deep water. On the west side—the side toward the pulp mill—there's a ramp going down to a float. Just be careful if you use a rowboat because sometimes strong winds can come up, and you might not be able to reach shore before choppy waves swamped your boat. The wet suits are hanging on a rod near the top of the ramp. Not many guests use them, but should you wish to do so, please feel free. We ask that before you return to your room you use the shower by the ramp to get all the salt water off."

The view from his balcony included the surface of Port Townsend Bay and the shoreline of Indian and Marrowstone Islands. He also could see much of the shore along Port Townsend. That area consisted of many docks and wharves. He noticed that most of the wharves rested on cement pilings. The wharf right next to the motel, though, did not have cement pilings. It had the old style, logs that years ago had been driven by a pile driver into the muck. On top of the wharf he saw a parking area near Water Street, and farther out over the water arose an old warehouse that appeared to be all boarded up. Between his balcony and the old wharf, something moved, and he looked and saw three otters surfacing and then diving again. Seaward, he recognized a loon sitting low. As he watched, the bird leaned forward and gracefully slipped under the water.

On a coffee table in his room lay a Seattle newspaper. Michael glanced at the headlines: "Federal Judge Orders Sewage Re-Route." That caught his attention. He read a few paragraphs of the lead article and learned that after a lengthy trial, environmental groups had obtained a federal court judgment protecting salmon by requiring that all sewage and street run-off no longer flow into Puget Sound. The order required that the fluids by piped to eastern Washington, there, to be cleansed by a new process: the sun evaporating the water to then condense along a separate drainage. The collected condensation would be pure water and would be piped back to Puget Sound as drinking water. The order allowed five years for implementation.

By now it was late afternoon. He felt in a hurry, but at the same time he wanted to relax. He sat in the hot tub for a while, long enough for the clouds to the southeast to move away. In their place he could see the Portage Canal Bridge, beyond it Mt. Rainier. By the time he finished dinner at the Lighthouse Cafe, darkness had set in. He walked by the old Victorian buildings along Water Street until he came to the beach at Point Hudson. Just off the point, the navigational buoy was lifting to a swell and making a harsh clanging sound. Its light flashed weakly, just bright enough to be seen by local marine traffic. As he walked along the beach he looked for the path to Chetzamoka Park. In the park he found the very swing he had used as a child. As he sat in it he could recall being pushed by his parents. Some memories were returning. Back on the beach, he walked by the old Fort Worden dock and remembered his parents teaching him to make the fifteen-foot jump off the dock. He recalled the trick: to only jump where one could get out of the cold water within seven seconds. Also, he remembered his father cautioning him to only jump in deep water, which had seemed like odd advice, until his father explained that if one jumped in shallow water, like, say, six feet deep, and hit the bottom, one could fracture his spine.

When he walked out on the dock he wondered where he had once actually stood before jumping. He knew it was where the water was deep. So much time had gone by, he could not decide where, as a child, he had jumped. When he walked the sandy beach to Point Wilson, he turned north and began walking west on the beach that ran along the Strait of Juan de Fuca. Swells came in, forming steep ridge lines that bent into collapsing curves that made a "thud" sound as each hit the sand. Then each wave escorted bubbles and pockets of foam up the beach, as if trying, quickly, to get Michael's shoes wet. He could hear seabirds. Upland, an owl hooted. As he walked he disturbed two oystercatchers; they rose in a loud squawking protest and flew away. At the westerly end of Fort Worden he entered a meadow and began to loop back. Even though it was dark, it was easy to follow the footpath that grooved the grass field. Soon, he walked by the sounds of bellowing marsh frogs. He walked to his grade school and circled the building. It looked exactly as it did when he had gone there. Just as when he was there, student drawings and finger paintings hung from the inside of the classroom windows.

He put off walking by his childhood home until last. It was there. The exterior had changed some, but it still had the lines of a pre-Victorian structure, more like a design copied from an 1850 common house from Maine. Inside the lights were still on. A trailer in the driveway held a runabout with a large outboard motor. In front of it was a new pick-up truck. Upon descending the concrete stairway he heard the seepage dripping and then, for the first time in years, recalled the lemonade stand—and his parents helping him build it. He sat on the bottom step for a while, thinking. While he rested there he thought back to the bizarre conduct of the people who had purchased the diluted lemonade.

Early the next day Michael left the motel to go hiking. He drove up to the Dungeness Valley into the Olympic National Forest to the trailhead to the Tubal Cain Mine. After walking the first three miles to the old mine, he kept on the trail for another two miles until he reached Buck Horn Lake. There he left the trail. He bushwhacked to the far side of the lake and slowly ascended a tumble of small rocks several hundred feet until he could see to his left a saddle in the mountain that ran to a small knoll. He traversed to the saddle and then crossed on over onto another scree. Looking across the scree, which was just a long rock slide resting in repose, up almost to the ridge line of the mountain, he saw a shape he remembered from before—what looked like a black door. Carefully, from rock to rock, he made his way up and across. The shape that from a distance looked like a doorway, was actually the rectangular entry to an exploratory horizontal mine shaft. Upon reaching the mine, he dropped his pack and removed from it some knee pads and a flashlight. He put on the pads. A few feet into the shaft the ground was covered with a slushy snow. About ten feet into the shaft, the snow hardened and even farther back the compacted snow changed to ice. The solid form of ice banked upwards until the crawlway was about eighteen inches below the ceiling of the shaft. Michael squirmed and slid along the top of the ice. Thousands of crystals of ceiling ice reflected the beam of his flashlight. Back 150 feet, the mine ended. People had scribbled their names or comments on the mine wall. Michael rolled onto his back and pointed his light straight up. There he saw once more the words his father had scraped: "Michael Storey and Joseph—1982."

Backing out of the shaft took some time. Descending the rockfalls demanded a good sense of balance. Where the two screes contained small rocks, Michael could stand there, shuffle his feet, and then commence to use his shoes as skis to slide down the hillside over many small rocks while remaining in a standing position. He had to be careful not to go too fast. Where the screes contained large rocks, Michael had to move from rock to rock, often using his hands to balance his body. Many rocks in each scree were just balanced in repose and the weight of Michael's body caused the rocks to roll down the scree. Sometimes half a dozen rocks were set loose and bounced and fell down the steep hillside. At one place in his descent he noticed a peculiar small rock. It was black with red circles. This was the type of rock he and his father had collected, orbicular jasper. They had broken such rocks with a sledge hammer to reduce their size and then placed the broken rocks in a lapidary tumbler. He now recalled the grumbling, tumbling sound of the tumbler—day after day, week after week. The finished stones shone with a high polish and were placed on the bottom of his goldfish tank. For the first time in years he recalled how lovely the finished stones were. Michael picked up the stone and put it in his pack.

At the lake, he removed his clothes and dove in. Concentric circles of waves formed from his movement and spread across the lake. Back on shore, he had no towel. All he could do was press his hands over his body, hoping he would dry faster. As he waited to dry he heard a "beep." He had heard it before but had forgotten what it was. Then he heard another "beep" and about twenty seconds later another. A second sound mixed in with the first: a sound like one would hear upon releasing air from a balloon. He knew it was a bird. His parents had told him what it was. He tracked the noises with his eyes. In the distance, far overhead, he recognized a nighthawk. It flitted about in the sky, almost directionless as a butterfly, and Michael saw it drop into a dive and plummet down. Its speed became so great that when it pulled out of the dive its wings, under considerable air pressure, fluttered and vibrated, making the deflating balloon sound. Such a strange bird, he recalled, for it only flies about for a short time each day, then about two hours before sunset. Down the trail later as Michael hiked out, he heard from time to time the two-tone call of the varied thrush.

By the time he reached his car it was dark. On the drive back he drove slowly, prepared to stop in case deer crossed the road. When he reached his motel a few minutes before midnight, he lay down and went to sleep.

XVII

During the night a shore wind commenced. The wind continued to pick up and by 3:00 A.M. the wind coming up Hood Canal had caused whitecaps to form on Port Townsend Bay. Rows of four-foot waves, fifty feet from crest to crest, formed on the bay and moved toward the Port Townsend beaches. Some of those waves advanced under and around the pilings under the Bay Motel. In the disturbed water under the motel, the waves lifted and pushed a log, causing it to pound against the concrete pilings. The sounds of the log beating the pilings awakened Michael Storey and kept him from returning to sleep. He dressed and went out on the balcony. The cold wind sharpened his senses. Seaward, out on the bay, he could see lines of white moving toward him, increasing in size as the waves neared. Then the white-capped waves slipped under the motel and slapped into the pilings and moved the log and then continued on into shallow water where the waves broke and receded. He noticed seagulls flying about the shoreline and he was surprised the birds could be nocturnal. Irritated by the sounds of the log, he left his room and walked to the westerly side of the motel where there was a ramp leading down to a little floating dock. The little dock was dancing to the storm waves. Waves lapped over its seaward edge. Springlines running from it to pilings kept it in place. Holding onto the ramp railings, he cautiously went down the ramp to discover whether he could see the log. He could. It was there under the motel, not too far from where he stood. He could see that the log was parallel to the beach and rubbing against two reinforced concrete pilings. Because the storm waves were approaching shore at a slight easterly angle, Michael guessed that if the log were pushed out from the motel it would be caught by the shore current and keep going. No one else appeared to be up. All the motel doors were closed and, where he could see windows, all the interior lights were off. He walked to the closet near the ramp that held the wet suits. There, he examined the wet suits and withdrew one that looked like it might fit. It had wrist and ankle zippers. He took off his clothes and began to put on the wet suit. It was like wrestling with a giant rubber band, but he got it on. Because no neoprene booties fit his feet, he decided to swim with his shoes on. He knew he had to wear something to protect his feet from kicking up against a piling covered with sharp barnacles. He found a hood. Back down the ramp he walked. When he sat on the edge of the bouncing float he could feel the seawater in his leather wingtipped shoes. As he lowered himself off the float, he could tell that the wet suit was loose simply by the quantity of cold water that flooded in. He thought of the contrast between being pleasantly asleep in the motel room and being in cold, thrashing water. In a moment the frigid water that had entered his wet suit warmed a bit from his body heat. He pushed away from the float and dog-paddled towards the log. He swam in a wave that crested and lifted him upwards towards the concrete base of the motel, then dropped him. Some waves topped and spilled over him. He did not feel afraid. He knew he could not sink because the air bubbles in the neoprene suit created more than enough buoyancy. As an epiphany of sorts, he realized he had been in situations like this before, as a child with his father. Before him he could see the dark hull of the log being pushed up against the pilings, falling back, and then being pushed again by a new wave. He knew if he got caught between the piling and the log he'd be crushed. He was also aware that, if he stayed at the end of the log and pushed and kicked, no harm would come to him. When he reached the log, a wave moved it away, toward the piling. "BAUUUUOOOOOMMMMM!" the log hit the piling and then bounced back into the fallen sea. Michael grabbed the end of the log and started to push it by kicking his legs. The log did not respond to his pressure. Then he kicked until a wave broke over him and the log, separating them. Now he was angry. He swam back and kick-pushed some more, but the log did not move toward the easterly side of the motel. Michael pulled up close to the end of the log and worked his feet up near the surface so he was in a bent-knee position, much as someone might be who was in an in-water starting position for a backstroke race. He then sprang away from the log, pushing his feet against the log. After three tries he noticed the log had moved. With continued effort, he pushed the log to where it was moving away. Approaching the log from downwind, Michael carefully inserted himself in the new space between the end of the log and a piling. He placed his hands on the log and his fancy shoes found traction on the sharp crowns of the piling barnacles. The log responded to his pressure. Once he created momentum in the log it kept going, until a new storm wave caught the log and pressed it up against another piling. Then the log stopped its lateral movement. Michael swam over and pushed anew. Finally, the log floated out from under the motel. Michael had no trouble swimming against the slight shore current. Back at the float he walked to just beyond the top of the ramp to find a firm place to stand. He undressed from the wet suit and rinsed his street shoes in fresh water while he showered. Gathering his clothing and, taking a chance, he walked naked along the motel hallways back to his room. There he dried his skin with towels and congratulated himself that the log noise had ceased. He lay down in bed to sleep and in a moment, "Beeeedle-Beeeedle-Beeeedle," his phone sounded.

"Hello?"

"Hello, Michael?"

"Yes, Pauline, this you?'

"Yes, sorry to bother you. We are three time zones ahead of you. Director Bones wants to talk with you."

"Hello, Michael, Bones here."

"Good morning, Director."

"Yes, good morning to you. I was wondering if you could return to headquarters today. We need you. This place is chaotic. I am getting flack from Congress."

Tempted though Michael was to simply say "Yes" and comply with the Director, he knew that if the Director was totally desperate he could order Michael back—and instead he had only inquired about his return. Michael elected to stay in Port Townsend a few days more.

"Look, Director Bones, this town where I am at is where I once lived but I have not been here for twenty-six years. My parents are buried here. I really would like a little time to be able to think of them in the context of where we all once lived. It seems like just by retracing my steps here, places I went with my parents, helps to rebuild a memory of them." That should soften his heart, thought Michael. Also, he knows I am one of the few at headquarters aware he is on pot.

"Well, OK, Michael. Do your best to return as soon as possible."

"Yes, sir."

"Goodby."

"Goodby."

He slept in. After breakfast at the Lighthouse Cafe, he rented a bicycle. Though he had walked around Fort Worden at night along the beach, he wanted to see the place during the day. Now a state park, at one time Fort Worden had served as headquarters for three forts defending Puget Sound from naval attack. The old guns had been designed to fire and to then hunch-back, to disappear on hinged carriages. With the advent of new weaponry, not the least of which was aircraft, the cannons and the forts became obsolete. Though the weapons had been removed, the huge concrete emplacements and mortar bunkers remained, as did many of the old, near-Victorian staff buildings. He biked along an asphalt road that led onto the bunker hill. Where once the hill had been cleared of vegetation to allow an unobstructed view of the sea lane, tall evergreen trees now stood, making the hill appear even higher. Where soldiers in concrete bunkers once looked out of horizontal slits for enemy ships, now canes of blackberry bushes arched out. He went to places he had gone with his parents to pick a small type of sweet

blackberry. He spotted the plants but he could tell the season for
the berries had passed. Vaguely, he recalled a place at Fort Worden
where there was an abandoned orchard, where his parents had
picked apples. He pedaled about the park looking, but he could
not find the orchard. At some distance he heard music, violins,
and as he bicycled closer to the fort barracks the sound increased.
When he turned onto a road that led behind the dining hall, he
saw several clusters of people sitting in circles on the grass. Some of
the musicians played guitars. Two held banjos. Three had mando-
lins. Most were cranking on violins. It was fiddle tune festival,
something he had totally forgotten about, but now, on hearing
the tunes, recalled, years ago, standing at Fort Worden with his
parents during fiddle festival concerts. His parents had saved the
entry fee by standing outside—and even there the fiddle sounds
had carried clearly.

Occasionally, someone would stand up, put away an instrument and walk away. Someone new would walk by a few minutes
later, sit down, open his instrument case, and join in playing a
tune. For a while Michael sat on a grass knoll, next to his bike,
listening. He would look at one group and try to isolate its tune
from all the other sounds. Then he would see if he could discern
the tune of another group. Two clusters played fiddle tunes. One
group was playing a waltz. Another presented a series of blues
tunes. The rest he could not differentiate.

Near him was stood an announcement board and on it were
tacked and taped different notices and bulletins. While still listening he walked over and examined the different sheets of paper.
One gave directions to a family reunion at a given campsite. Another offered information about the Marine Science Center. Then
Michael glanced at one and read it a second time. It was a schedule for a convention of morticians. It announced that at 1:00 P.M.
in the old theater building there would be a lecture about the
"Lady of the Lake." That title tweeked his curiosity. He decided to
bike down to the lighthouse and back and then to see if he could
get permission to attend whatever the lecture was about.

"No, sorry, sir, you do not have a badge, you cannot come in. This lecture is for morticians, only."

"Well, ummm," countered Michael, as he reached for his wallet, "would this do?" The doorman thought Michael would just walk away, and he was hesitant to be bothered by him. He glanced at the card: "MICHAEL STOREY, UNITED STATES FEDERAL BUREAU OF INVESTIGATION, ASSISTANT TO DIRECTOR RICHARDSON BONES."

"OK. Come in. There's lots of room anyway. Most of the convention-goers are playing golf."

Inside, Michael sat down in the back. Rows of seats ahead slightly angled down to a stage. He could see that the theater had been built in a time before cinema. That explained the large stage at the front. On that platform he noticed a morgue-like table. On top was a body covered with a shroud. A foot stuck out.

"Ladies and gentlemen, can you hear me?'

People ahead of Michael nodded affirmatively.

"Well, I'd like to thank you for being here today. As you can see, many of the convention-goers are not here. I can assure you that is their loss as the lecture you are about to hear is a bit unusual."

He continued: "The topic today is body saponification. Saponification describes the situation where the human body over time changes chemically to allow the cadaver to retain its life-like appearance and to attain a consistency of soap, or like that of lard. I doubt any of us will come across this situation during our entire time of serving society as morticians."

"Boring," Michael thought to himself and he criticized his own curiosity for taking him away from being outdoors. He leaned forward to rise and to leave when he noticed the speaker's hand move to lift the shroud. Again, his curiosity got the better of him and he sat back.

"This actually is not a real body. It is a model of a cadaver that I created by mixing lard and soap together with chemical drying accelerants. I used a knife to carve the final form to look like the human cadaver you see.

"Now, the scene is set. All we need is an explanation. Ladies and gentlemen, I now want to introduce to you, Officer Fred Happer. Officer Happer is retired from the Clallam County Sheriff's Office. That would be west of here, where Port Angeles is the county seat. Please welcome Officer Happer."

The room filled with the sound of people clapping their hands, but after the applause ended, no one came to the stage. Michael glanced around and he noticed movement in the front row. Slowly, an old man struggled up to a standing position. He had a walker and an oxygen tank along one side. He moved the walker, then his feet, then extended the walker further, leaned ahead to place his body weight on it and then his feet stepped forward, almost like an inch worm. When he came to the two steps to the level of the stage, people in the audience rose and helped him. Upon reaching the microphone he turned toward the audience and Michael could see a gray plastic tube running from the oxygen to the speaker's nostrils. Then there was a brief commotion on the stage as the podium was replaced by a low table. A chair was carried forward from back stage to allow the speaker to sit down during his presentation.

Wrinkles rippled across his weathered face. As he started to speak his voice sounded weak, as though he had not enough air to sound his words. He pulled the microphone closer to his mouth.

"Hello, y'll. My name is Fred Happer. Glad to be here. Now, I don't want any of you rushing up here and forcing embalming fluid down me." He chuckled at his own joke; the audience did not take easy to being made fun of. One person groaned.

"I'm invited here to tell you something that happened years ago when I was a young man. In December, 1937, we had a missing woman in Clallam County. Her neighbors had reported to the sheriff that they had not seen her for some time. Her husband explained he and she had argued so often that one day she got on a bus going east and made no further contact. We opened a file, but there was not much to put in it. Then, in the summer of 1940, at Lake Crescent, not too far west from Port Angeles, fishermen found a body wrapped in blankets and floating. They called for help and I was one of the deputies sent to investigate. When I got there the body was still floating next to the boat ramp. The first thing I noticed was that the body and blankets were tied together, bundled, if you would, with rotten rope. It was clear someone had used rocks to sink the body and that some time later the rope had rotted or weakened from moisture—and the body and the blankets had floated to the top of the lake. I had to wade in with a hand dolly. We positioned the corpse over it and then pulled the dolly up the loading ramp to the ambulance. Later, at the county morgue, I stood there while the county coroner removed the rest of the ropes and then the blankets. What we saw was a surprise. The body, that of a young woman, had changed in its chemical texture or makeup to appear exactly like a white marble statue. She had turned to soap. Her face looked just as it appeared before she died. Her flesh felt firm. Due to some exposure to certain chemicals at the bottom of Lake Crescent the body had not decayed. Neighbors of the missing woman were called in to view the body and each confirmed the identity of the cadaver as that of the missing woman. At that point the husband's story did not hold together, and he was charged with murder. A jury agreed and the killer was packed off to prison."

The old man had told his story. The master of ceremonies thanked him. The gathering was over almost as quickly as it had commenced. Outside again, Michael lay about listening to fiddle tunes. Later, he pedaled over to San Juan Avenue, to 19th, then to Kearney, then along Water Street to return the bicycle to the bike shop and to retrieve his deposit. That evening he went from tavern to tavern, sipping on apple juice. He looked for anyone he might recognize from the past. No one looked familiar.

XVIII

That night Michael Storey should have slept well. Unlike the evening before, there was no wind. Port Townsend Bay had no waves. No log banged against the motel pilings. Still, he could not sleep. For a while he lay in bed and in the darkness listened to National Public Radio. Then he got out of bed and went to the balcony. He saw that the tide was out. He looked over at the old wharf. It looked abandoned, boarded up, no lights on, no cars in its parking area. Below the old wharf, long wooden pilings were exposed by the low tide. Marine growths hanging on the pilings gave the logs the look of being wider than they were. Again, he noticed seagulls flying near the motel, then circling into darkness. When he realized he could not sleep he wondered if he should pack up, drive to Sea-Tac airport, and catch an early flight back to Washington, D.C.

Not certain why, he decided to leave his motel room and see if he could get enough gear together to snorkel along the shoreline. He had no difficulty in finding the wet suit worn the night before. If he went back in the water he knew he would have to wear his still-wet wingtipped shoes. This time, though, he would put on an extra two pairs of socks before putting on the shoes. He needed a waterproof flashlight. He wondered what to do for such a light. Leaving the motel he drove to a gas station and purchased four flashlights, eight "D" cell batteries, and two rolls of electrical tape. Then he went to an all-night supermarket, and in the produce department he found a roll of clear plastic sacks. He removed four long sacks. At the counter the clerk looked in surprise at the empty sacks and said there'd be no charge. Back in the car he placed two batteries in each flashlight and then made certain each worked.

He placed the flashlights side by side, with each switch facing outwards, and used the electrical tape to bundle them together. He placed the flashlights in the plastic sack, twisted the open end of the sack, and then double-backed the end over the twist before circling it with electrical tape to be double sure the sack was watertight. Then he repeated placing and wrapping each of the three remaining plastic sacks. Four sacks, he thought, that should be enough to keep the batteries dry. He then circled electrical tape around the sides and the ends of the wrapped flashlights in a way that created a handle loop on one side.

Back at the motel he left his car keys and his wallet in his room. At the ramp, he undressed and put on the wet suit. On the shelf in the wet suit closet lay a cheap face mask and a child's snorkel breathing tube. With the wet suit on, he sat down and replaced his socks and his shoes. On the closet floor, in a corner, he hid the plastic card that served as a room key. After adjusting the face mask strap, he decided to turn on the shower. He let the hot water flow onto his neck and then down into his wet suit. This way he would not have to feel the cold water entering his wet suit. Instead, the hot shower water got there first. As he walked down the ramp water drained out of the bottom of the wet suit and he looked like an oddly-formed, leaking balloon. But when he lowered himself into the salt water there was no shocking discomfort of cold water except on his exposed hands and the area of his forehead between the top of the face mask and the edge of the wet suit hood. At first he simply floated with his head down in the water and saw nothing except the color black. When he pressed through the four layers of plastic sacks, one flashlight turned on and a dull glow appeared within the translucent sacks. Slowly, as he turned on the other flashlights, the water around him became brighter. Little bits of plankton reflected back the brilliance. The shore current carried Michael away from the float, easterly along the shoreline. Vaguely, the bottom appeared below. He swam toward shore so he could see the bottom closer. Then he floated, letting the current move him along. The slow shore current treated him to changing scenes of different patches of seaweed, eelgrass, and shrub-like brown algae. He could see shrimp eyes reflecting light. Small crabs scurried about below him. Little eels snaked along near the bottom. He realized that this part of Port Townsend was not at all asleep. Some junk lay there. He saw a rusted auto wheel and realized it still retained its wooden spokes. Beer bottles were frequent. Some of the bottles sported barnacles and clumps of bright-green seaweed. One type of seaweed showed off iridescent colors. Another had little bags that were pocked with tapioca-like dimples on the outside and contained pockets of chambered air on the inside.

Suddenly, just below Michael, his light was blocked by what appeared as a huge swimming, bright yellow, chicken egg yolk. Michael recognized it as a giant poisonous jellyfish. Its sides spread out like wings, and then, in unison, contracted downward, propelling the jellyfish in the opposite direction. Its twenty-inch-diameter flat top was at an angle, allowing it to swim across the shore current. Michael could see the long, poisonous tentacles extending many feet down below the jellyfish. He made no move. He just lay there in the water while the current carried him and the jellyfish. Slowly, the jellyfish moved from a few feet below him to deeper water.

In a moment his flashlight illuminated what looked like a giant elephant leg. He had reached a piling supporting part of the old wharf. The tide was so low that most of the growths on the piling, like giant barnacles, California mussels, and piling worms, remained high and dry above Michael. As he floated under the wharf he saw a wide line of white on the bottom. When he was directly over them he recognized the large tubular bodies of sea anemones. Their outer circle of tentacles made them look like delicate flowers.

Enough water had seeped in and out of Michael's wet suit that he felt chilled. He wondered how much longer he should remain in the water. As he floated by a broken piling that rested at a steep angle, something long and dark moved toward his face mask. It had fangs, big eyes, and appeared very ugly. It was a muscular nine-foot wolf eel. It could easily bite off his thyroid. Years ago Michael had read in a diving magazine that the wolf eel is actually docile and likes to be petted. Slowly he moved his hand to the top of the fish and then he gently stroked the fish's skin. "So far, so good," he thought. In a few minutes the eel turned and flanked its long body by Michael and disappeared.

By this time Michael was cold. He had had enough. Still under the old wharf, he began to kick his feet to swim towards shore. Slowly, the water became shallow. When the depth was about five feet, the bottom changed to rocks and he saw below a multitude of different colored starfish. Then he noticed a bottom mound covered with reddish rock crabs. Hustling about, the crabs appeared to be eating something. Michael knew the mound could not be the remains of a dead seal or sea lion because such bodies contained so much fat they would float. The mound was too big to be a dead fish, like a king salmon. Michael wanted a closer look. He made a surface dive. The rock crabs took note of the light, sensed movement, and scurried off the mound. He ran his hand into the mound. It felt like the mound held small pieces of heavy wood. A muddy turbulence arose and blocked his view. He was out of breath anyway and let the buoyancy of the wet suit lift him back to the surface. He took a breath of fresh air and prepared for a second dive. The shore current moved the cloud of turbid water away. He had to kick to regain his position, and then he tucked his body and raised his legs above the water to force his body down. This time, with his free hand, he grabbed pieces from the mound and returned to the surface. "Bones!" He recognized pieces of bones. "Can't be too old," he thought, "or the crabs would not be interested." One bone was discolored and old, but another bone he had grabbed deep within the pile looked meat-market fresh. Michael suspected that the contents of the pile must have been dropped from above. He beamed his flashlight upwards to the old wharf and he saw directly overhead a hole in the floor, a drop chute.

He decided to collect samples to inspect at the motel room.

He had no pockets. His fingers felt numb. Slowly he pulled on the
wet suit jacket zipper and moved it down several inches. Cold
water followed, but by then the temperature change did not faze
him. He reached up and inserted the bones inside his wet suit.
Then he dove for more. After six dives he had twenty samples,
contributing to a bulge in his wet suit. Feeling uncomfortably
cold he swam toward shore. When he reached the beach he
clambered over beach logs and then up seawall steps to the sidewalk.
From there it was a short distance back to the motel. He left a trail
of seawater along the sidewalk. The contracting pressure of the wet
suit pulled the bones against his own stomach—and there must
have been a small crab within the hollow of one bone—for he
could feel something walking over his skin and then pinching him—
and it was most unpleasant. At the motel he took a side entry and
was soon getting out of the wet suit in the shower near the ramp.
This time he had a towel handy. He dried and then put on his
clothes. With his fingers he ripped holes in the plastic walls of his
flashlight bundle and then he removed the flashlights and inserted
the bones. In the motel room he spilled the bones into the bathroom
sink and then filled the rest of the sink with luke warm water. He
saw the crab that had been on his stomach and he grabbed it and
walked across the room and tossed it from the balcony. He looked
at the motel radio clock—3:43 A.M. Energized from the swim, he
did not feel tired. He reached down into the sink and pulled out a
bone. He could tell it was not from a bird. Though the bone had
a thickness of about an inch, he knew it was not large enough to be
from a cow, or a bull, or a horse, elk, or bear. He examined different
pieces. Strange, he thought. Something felt very odd. The bones
looked like bones he had seen before. What? Most of the bones
appeared to have cutting lines created by a butcher's band saw.
Those cut lines ran uniformly parallel. He held a bone that on
one end had the band saw marks. The other cut end was
different. Its surface was smoothly flush, with the exception of
three parallel groves. The groove in the middle ran shallow, but
the grooves on each side of it were at least a sixteenth of an inch

deep. He found three more bones that had the same exact groove pattern.

A memory of conversation at FBI headquarters crossed his mind. He reached for his cellular phone.

"Hello, FBI."

"Yes, this is agent Michael Storey; please, could you put me through to the forensics lab?"

"Please hold."

In a few minutes Michael heard: "Lab."

"Yes, this is Michael Storey, Assistant to Director Bones. Please tell me who you are."

"Judith Winder."

"Yes, I know you. We have talked before."

"Yes, how can I help you?"

"You may know that we are working on cases of young men who have recently disappeared. As part of that inquiry we are studying human remains found recently at different places in the United States."

"Yes, I am familiar with that."

"Of the bones recovered, did not all of them have the same marks? I mean, where the bones were cut, it looked like a shear was used, but it also seemed, I believe, that the shear marks had a pattern that appeared on each bone—as though part of the shear blade had some nicks or notches."

"Let me check. May I phone you back in a few minutes?"

"Yes."

Five minutes later they were back on the phone.

"Yes," said Judith, "there is a bone pattern. It consists of three parallel grooves. The middle groove is not too pronounced but the grooves to each side are deeper, about a sixteenth of an inch. Is that what you wanted to know?"

"Yes, thank you for your help."

Michael stared at the bones. Not for an instant did he think he had discovered anything. Chances are the machine that made the shears was itself defective and caused many shears to have the same imperfection. He walked to the balcony railing and looked over at the dark old wharf.

"Just what is inside?" he asked himself.

XIX

"Surely," Michael thought, "there must be some way to look around inside that old building." He decided to use the pre-dawn darkness to check out the building. Quickly, he left the motel and walked to the parking lot on the old wharf. No cars were parked there and the wharf building appeared dark and unoccupied. The windowless shoreward exterior wall of the old wharf building ran from one side of the dock to the other. There was no way to walk from the parking area along the outer sides of the structure. Michael saw no traffic coming along Water Street and no early-morning walkers coming his way. He walked across the parking area toward a large door. He tried to move the door's handle and it did not budge. Locked. On the wall next to the door was a small sign and Michael took out his flashlight and used its light to read the sign: "PRIVATE PROPERTY. NO TRESPASSING. STAY AWAY. P.T.M.C."

He guessed at what the abbreviation might stand for: "Port Townsend Men's Club? Port Townsend Machinists' Club? What?"

He stood back and stared at the building. It had the lines of an early-day cannery building. Originally, daylight reached the workers inside by way of vertical walls of windows along a clerestory that ran the length of the building. Now those windows were boarded over by sheets of plywood. Michael returned to the motel and walked down the ramp to the float. There, he inspected a rowboat while bailing it free of rainwater. He tested the oars in the oarlocks. Things seemed to work. It was a wooden boat, about ten feet long. No one had cared for it for some time, but it looked like it would hold him. He untied the painter and pushed the craft away from the float. Carefully, he rowed between the motel pilings and then out into the open water between the motel and the old wharf. The dock of the old wharf extended seaward about twenty feet beyond the wharf building. Michael rowed toward that apron to see if there were a ladder. Sure enough, on the far side a crusty, battered, steel ladder dangled down from what seemed like its last holding bolt. When new it must have looked sharp. Then, the ladder metal rungs of the straight ladder would have advanced in a rectangular pattern down into the water. Over the years it had been rammed and pushed by vessels tying up alongside it and by logs caught in storm waves. As Michael rowed up against the ladder, it looked ready to fall at any time. Michael tied the painter rope to it anyway. The tide was still out. He noticed the rungs were encrusted with barnacles and lumps of mussels. He had thought ahead and brought a pair of thick gloves, which he then put on. He shipped his oars. When his body weight shifted from the rowboat, the ladder swung backwards under the dock. If it had broken loose just then, it would have fallen over Michael and pinned him on the bottom of the bay. From rung to rung he worked his way up. Above sea level the rungs were free of clinging sea life and were easy to grasp. He pulled himself over the bullrail of the dock and quickly walked to the door there. It was locked. The building had no other doors and no windows along its first floor level. Above, where the clerestory ended, Michael saw a broken window. A flat wooden wall of twenty feet separated him from the window and there was no ladder lying on the dock. He stared at the broken window. Maybe the wind had blown off the plywood that once covered it. Maybe, just to allow some natural light in, it had never been boarded over.

He knew he could get in the building through that window if he could reach it. From the ferry dock, two wharves away, Michael heard the diesel engines kick in. Soon the ferry would be making its first run for the day. That reminded Michael that dawn approached and that he should be on his way. While he returned to the rowboat he wondered how he might reach that window. He could rent a twenty-foot ladder, but his car had no overhead rack, and such a ladder near the motel would raise too many questions.

Back at the motel, when Michael was leaving to get some breakfast, he heard the desk clerk:

"Excuse me, Sir. Mr. Michael Storey, I believe. Sorry to bother you but there is a message for you marked 'urgent.'" She handed over a slip of paper and Michael recognized the phone number of Director Bones. He returned to his room and put through the call.

"Pauline? Michael here. I got a message to call. What is up?"

"Michael, thanks for phoning in. Some congressmen are threatening a hearing if we do not explain why so many young men are missing. The Justice Department is wondering why we are not making any arrests. Some parents have connected and are planning to picket outside until we explain what happened to their sons. Here, I will get Director Bones. He is out on the balcony smoking a joint."

"Michael, things are getting out of hand back here. I am sorry but I am ordering you to return today, this morning, now. Then you can help me as soon as this afternoon."

Michael was not certain what to say. He did not want to make a fool of himself, but at the same time he wished to stall for time to at least look inside of that old building.

"Sir, if you order me back and if I then tell you what I have found here, you will send me back to Port Townsend."

"Say what?" the director responded. "What do you mean?"

Michael looked down at his soggy-looking shoes and then he explained to the director the markings on the bones he had found.

Following a long silence at the other end of the phone, the director asked:

"If you do stay, what are your intentions?"

"I'd like to break into the building to see what is there."

Again there was a long silence.

"OK, Michael, give it a try. Do you want any backup?"

"No."

"OK. Just be careful. Stay a day or two. Keep in touch at least twice a day. Before you break in, I suggest you learn as much as you can about the interior of the building. For example, if there is a local museum, go there and ask about the history of the building. Maybe the structure is on the tax rolls; see the assessor and ask to look at their records. To know the valuation of the building they might have to go inside once in a while. Leave your I.D. at the motel. If you get in a spot we will help you from the top down. Good luck."

Richardson Bones placed the phone down. He stared at the wall for a few minutes and then he picked up the phone and buzzed his secretary.

"Pauline, could you please do something for me? I'd like you to contact the lab and ask that the groove pattern on some of the bones of what we believe to be one or more of the missing young men, well, I'd like you to get the lab to photograph the groove pattern on some of the bone ends and to then fax those photographs to companies that manufacture shears. With the fax send a simple question, namely, ask if the pattern is common to most shear cuts."

"Yes, sir."

One hour later replies began coming in. Each manufacturer reported that all new shears made a clean cut. Several responses suggested that the groove pattern in the faxed photographs could only be made by one set of shears.

During lunch time, Director Bones again buzzed Pauline.

"Pauline, do you remember that fellow that called the office from Colorado, the grade school friend of mine who was crying, whose son had disappeared?"

"Yes, Director Bones."

"Well, I owe him a favor. Michael may be up to something in Port Townsend, Washington, and may need some help. I would like you to phone Denver and ask the agents there to contact Benny Edwards and his wife, Gudrun, I believe, and to somehow have them at the Denver airport at 8:00 tonight. Mountain Time. Tell Benny they should be packed for being away for a couple days."

"Will do," Pauline responded.

"Also, Pauline, you pack up, too. You and I are taking an FBI plane west. We will stop at Denver to pick up Benny and his wife. Spread the word that I have gone away on an emergency. I hope you can be away for a couple days."

"No problem," she replied as she looked at many files on her desk, the tabs of paper evidencing phone calls still to be returned, and the photograph of her three kids and husband.

"Thank you," said Bones. "We are going to Port Townsend."

XX

Tired. He'd been up all night. He walked over to the Lighthouse Cafe for breakfast. Back at the motel he stopped at the front desk long enough to arrange to stay two more days. In his mind no solution had formed as to how to reach the wharf window. He decided to sleep on it. In the motel room he pulled the window shades to block out the sun. Against FBI rules, he deactivated his cellular phone. He slept into the afternoon. While lying in darkness he mulled over how to reach the window—and slowly a way came to mind.

"All I need is a hardware store," he told himself.

He recalled seeing a hardware store just outside downtown Port Townsend, but he elected to walk by the many tourist stores in the historical district in the firm belief or hope that somewhere within the old buildings there remained a hardware store. Sure enough, on Water Street, just between Taylor and Adams Streets, he saw a sign: "Jefferson Hardware." Just below that sign he saw an unwashed stained glass window that had itself once been a sign and presented one word: "Delmonico." Before entering he glanced at the old Victorian brick wall. The bead joints between the bricks were just too straight, too parallel, too perfect. He took out a key and scratched one black bead mortar joint line and, sure enough, the surface behind was not more mortar, but, instead, the solid wall of a brick. "A fake finish," he realized.

"Yes sir, how are you today?" The girl asking the question looked like she was still in grade school. Even the cash register next to her looked bigger than she did and was certainly heavier. Michael looked around for someone older and then said to the young lady, "Please, I'd like to purchase a portable drill kit that includes a battery, a charger, and then seven more batteries and some screws. Oh, excuse me, I'd also like some barn door handles and some dark brown paint in a spray can."

She showed him the bin of screws and let him pick what he wanted while she went for the drill kit, the extra batteries, and the paint. She tabulated the cost and asked him to pay. "Barn door handles, if we have them, might be in the back. If so, you can pay for them on your way out. Just go through that doorway back there and ask my grandfather."

Upon passing through the doorway, Michael entered a long hallway. At its end were two doors. He walked down the hallway and opened the wrong door. As soon as he entered, a voice said, "Sit down."

"Where?" wondered Michael, for the room was dark, filled with smoke, and the only light was an incandescent bulb hanging at an angle from a long ceiling wire. The bulb illuminated a card table covered with a green felt cloth. Five men sat around the table. No one looked at him. They were looking at their cards.

The dealer glanced up and repeated himself: "Sit down." He pointed at a sixth chair beside the card table. When Michael sat, nothing more was said to him. It seemed as though he were not there. Suddenly, the dealer leaned forward and picked up all the cards. While he shuffled them he said to Michael, "Twenty dollar limit. No checks. No IOU's." Michael had not gambled at cards since the lunch breaks at FBI school. He did not even know what they were playing. He said nothing. The dealer dealt each player one card, then a second card. The dealer's second card was placed face up.

The man to the dealer's left said, "Five dollars," and placed a five-dollar bill on the table.

The next man said, "Two dollars," and placed two dollar bills on the table.

Uncertain, Michael said, "Five dollars," and pulled one from his wallet and dropped it on the table. His mind raced, trying to recall how to play the game. He remembered that it was called Twenty-One or Blackjack.

After the bidding the dealer asked in rotation if any player wished to take a hit, another card. Michael passed. His two cards added up to 19. He glanced at the other players. One, a bald gentleman with a roundish face, sat upright with a generous stomach pushed up against the table. His potbelly stretched at the fibers of his white T-shirt to the point where Michael could see the darker coloration of skin. The card player to Michael's right wore a formal suit. Clean tie. Clean shave. Fresh white formal shirt. Gold-rimmed glasses. All the trimmings for what he was: the Jefferson County Prosecutor. Another man, as skinny as a rail, nursed a whiskey bottle. His skin appeared jaundiced. He looked like he had not had a meal in years. No one spoke to Michael. Mostly, they eyeballed their cards. The fourth person broke the silence and just kept talking. He was not talking to anyone in particular. As he spoke he would think of a funny twist to what he was saying and then say it and break out in laughter, laughing at his own remark. When the dealer asked him for a bid, the talkative man would ask the dealer to repeat himself. Michael guessed he had a hearing problem. As he listened, Michael realized that what the talkative man uttered was in fact truly funny. Maybe he entertained himself by his own sense of irony and humor.

The dealer's eyes moved quickly from player to player. No one wanted any more cards. The dealer turned up two tens and cleared the money off the table, including Michael's five dollars. In twenty minutes Michael was down forty dollars. The drunk cast his eyes up to Michael and said: "Who are you?"

"Michael Storey."

The drunk looked him over a second time and mumbled to himself, "Storey, used to know one, years ago in school."

"Joe?" asked Michael.

At that the drunk sat straight and stared right at Michael. "Why, yes, how'd you guess?"

"My father. I'm here on vacation; have not been around for many years." When he explained who he was, the card game slowed, for each of the other players seemed to be deep in thought.

"We all knew your parents," offered the prosecutor. "We all went to school together. Your dad, your mom, Sandy, they were once part of our lives. Fine people. We even knew their parents. Shame the way the county let that turnoff remain so dangerous so many years. After the lawsuit by your parents' estate the judge was so irate he ordered the commissioners into his chambers and told them off until the walls turned blue. Next year the county removed the blind curve."

The heavyset man put his cards down for a moment and looked into the cloud of cigarette smoke just above his head and remarked, "My parents owned a bus line in town and your dad and I would get free rides to Quilcene. Then we'd hike up the Big Quilcene to Marmot Pass and hang out there until our food gave out. One time we even made it to Charlia Lakes. Best times I ever had in my life were being lost in the mountains with your father. One time I was ahead and accidentally stepped on a ground hive of bees. Your father followed and walked right into the agitated bees. Man, he was stung all over his face and arms. We broke off tree branches and swatted the attacking bees while we ran toward a nearby lake. Your father sat in the lake while I placed cool mud over his skin."

The drunk tested his memory, saying, "Your mother's sister married my uncle's stepson. Oh, what was his name?"

"Martin Williams, married to April," answered Michael. "They raised me, after my parents passed away, on the East Coast."

"Yes, so we are related! Cousins, maybe?" He stood at the table and reached across to shake Michael's hand. Michael, too, rose. As they shook hands a strong breath of whiskey encircled Michael. He turned to the others and thanked them for allowing him to play cards and said he had to leave. Without looking at him they said goodby. Each of the players was eagerly looking at the cards being dealt.

Back in the hallway, Michael approached the second door. It opened to a large storage room lined with shelves and bins. "Hello," he said loudly as he entered. No one answered. In the middle of the room was a desk and Michael walked toward it. As he approached he saw the form of a man crumpled over the desk. Getting closer, Michael determined that the man was actually sitting on a chair and that his chest and head lay on the top of the desk.

"Hello!" he repeated. No movement.

Michael came close to the man's ear and repeated himself. The body on the desk moved slightly and a weak voice said: "Be with you shortly. Have to get the blood flowing." The man's arms moved slowly across the top of the desk, almost like the legs of an octopus unfolding. The head remained down on the desk. One hand circled a lightbulb on a short table lamp on the desk. The other hand reached toward the same table lamp and its fingers pried at a switch and clicked it. Then both hands cupped the lightbulb. Michael saw the bulb's light passing through the translucent flesh of the skinny, yellowish fingers.

Without moving, the old man said: "Sorry to keep you. Just take a minute for me to get fired up." For several minutes Michael remained standing next to the desk while the old man gathered heat from the lightbulb. As soon as the coloration of the fingers changed to a bright pink the man sat up and asked how he might be helpful.

"Please, I'd like twenty metal barn door handles, as large as you have." The old man rose from his chair. His body leaned forward as though his back were out. Taking small steps, he disappeared behind some tall shelves and Michael could hear him sliding boxes about. In a moment he returned with what Michael wanted. He made out a billing statement and handed it to Michael. When Michael reached for the door to leave, he glanced back at the desk. The old man had already sat down and had set his arms and head down on the desk top to rest anew.

At the cashier he mentioned he had taken the wrong door. "Who are those people playing cards?"

She answered: "Just local people who play cards each afternoon. The prosecuting attorney. A real estate agent. A bus driver. The skinny man with the liquor bottle, he is from here. He owns this place. He is my dad. It is his father you met to make this purchase. The dealer you saw, well, he is a mortician from Quilcene. Comes every day and stays unless he gets a body call. I buy most of my clothing from his secondhand store at lower Port Haddock. He has a lot of irons in the fire, many investments, but almost each day he makes it here.

Michael dropped his purchases at the motel and then walked to the Jefferson County courthouse. Built in 1893 with brick from Milwaukee, the three-story structure at one end was a tall bell tower with a clock near the top. Every sixty minutes the bell sounded the hour. Originally the basement had served as a jail, but now new rooms provided space for the County Planning Department. As he walked by the monkey puzzle tree on the courthouse lawn, the tower bell sounded four times.

From across an oak counter, an assistant to the assessor faced Michael and asked how he might be helped.

"I am a tourist with some time on my hands. I am wondering if you could please give me information about a wharf downtown. It is just east of the Bay Motel, where I am presently staying."

"Certainly; let me figure the legal description from the city plat, and then we can look up the parcel on the assessor's rolls."

In a moment she returned. She typed a code on her keyboard. In a flash her computer screen showed a schematic drawing of the wharf.

"This shows the boundaries and improvements to the property. It is two dollars a page for a printout, if you wish."

He paid. In the hall he sat on a bench and looked at two sheets of paper. One page showed the assessed valuation and named the property owner as P.T.M.C., Inc., a Delaware corporation, having a Delaware post office box number for an address.

The second page provided an interior sketch. It showed that the seaward two-thirds of the building comprised one big meeting room. The remaining one-third served as an entry hallway, bathrooms, and a kitchen. The cooking area looked enormous as if it had banquet capacity. It had long food preparation tables and a

big walk-in freezer next to a walk-in cooler. Near one kitchen wall
he saw a row of lines suggesting a stairway. On the sheet he read,
"Ceiling lowered 2004 and now clerestory space is an attic that
runs length of building." That would do, thought Michael. If I
can get through the broken window I can walk in the attic. Maybe
I can get to the stairway to learn what is in the rest of the building.

From the courthouse he walked along Washington Street downtown to the local museum. As he entered, a lady welcomed him
and asked that he sign the guest book and to pay a suggested
donation of two dollars. He did both and then turned to walk
through the museum. The place reeked of history. Victorian furni-
ture. Indian implements and clothing. In one corner was a square
grand piano that had left New York in 1867 on a sailing ship that
had gone south around South America before unloading the piano
at Port Townsend. In the basement he walked through jail cells. In
an adjoining room was a layout of where the old logging railroads
had run on the east side of the Olympic Peninsula. He stared at an
early dental drill that operated by a footpedal. Upstairs, in the
research library, a well-dressed man greeted Michael and offered
to be of any assistance.

"Well, yes, thank you; there's an old wharf in town that I am
curious about. It is just east of the Bay Motel."

"Oh, sure, we can help. We have files on the different buildings within the historical district." He motioned Michael to sit
down at a large table and he walked over to some filing cabinets
and pulled a top drawer.

"This dock has a special history. It is perhaps the oldest dock
in Puget Sound. As far as we can tell it was built one year after the
American Civil War, 1866. Originally it was used for outfitting
sailing ships. The building contained tons of sailcloth, miles of
hemp rope, pulleys, turnbuckles, galley stores; whatever allowed a
ship to stay at sea. When Seattle and Tacoma outpaced Port
Townsend in commerce, the building went through different owners, each one putting the wharf to a new use. At one time it was a
salmon cannery. On another occasion it was a cannery for sea cu-

cumbers, later a cannery for clams and then true cod. One operator rendered the livers of dogfish for oil and it was closed down because of the rancid smell. For a while it looked like a railroad might establish a transcontinental terminal at Port Townsend, and in the hope of that happening some investors bought the wharf to use for unloading and storing coal. Recently it served as an ice house to provide ice to commercial fishermen. Five years ago it was purchased by a Delaware corporation. Just after that many construction workers appeared from out of town and went to work remaking the interior. Walls were removed. The light from the windows banking the clerestory was blocked by a lowered ceiling. All the exterior windows were covered over with sheets of wood. It was odd because no local people were hired to work there. It did not make sense to me to improve the interior and then to board up the place. Why? We tried to meet the officers of the corporation that owned the wharf but no one replied to our letters. We even attempted to walk into the building while it was under reconstruction. They told us to leave. We did the next best thing: we went to the city and bought a copy of the building permit application which included schematic drawings of the intended improvements. We know now that a meeting hall was built in part of the interior and a large kitchen elsewhere."

Michael asked: "So who are the owners?"

"We do not know. They go by a corporate acronym: PTMC. Rumor has it that the owners are some sort of an exclusive club and that the club meets in the building once a year, about now. As far as we can tell, no one in Jefferson County is a member of that club."

"Were there many other wharves in Port Townsend?'

"Yes, a good number. Some burned down. Some were torn down. Most fell down."

"Fell down? How would that be?"

"Mostly by ignorance. From what we know now, a wood boring worm at the early stages of its life swims in saltwater. At that stage of its life it seeks out wood to live in, in the case of wharves, the log pilings that support the main dock. It is sort of like a microscopic clam that can swim alongside wood, attach itself to the wood, and then can rub its outer shell against the wood to make a tiny hole. It enters the hole and its outer shell develops more lines of hard notches. The two shells do not stay still like for a normal clam. Instead, muscles in the worm work the shells back and forth, call it flapping, if you will, and the notches scratch against the wood rasping it and creating a tunnel way for the worm. Although the entry hole remains very small, the worm inside the wood increases in size. While it is hidden from sight, it rasps and eats its way inside the wood until the log is so hollow that the piling strength is lost. Eventually many pilings would be weakened and the dock would collapse. I forget the Latin name, but the common name for the invasive mollusk is 'teredo.'"

"So why," Michael asked, "didn't the PTMC wharf fall down years ago? Chances are those old pilings did not have any creosote to even try to block teredos."

"That I can answer. We have the diary of the first owner. He had examined logs on the beach and he had used an ax to open them up to see the interior teredo holes. He then took a log that had been afloat for some time and he pulled it ashore and cut it open. With this log he could view living teredos. From his examination he realized that a teredo is just a type of clam that looks like a worm but has two shells at its forward end. On the surface of each shell he saw hard notches. He could see the exposed teredos constantly moving the shells on their hinges, back and forth and back and forth, without any rest. He innovated a method to stop teredos. First he paid fishermen to catch thousands of dogfish and to provide him with the livers. He rendered the livers until he had hundreds of gallons of dogfish oil. Then he took the logs that he intended to use for a wharf and he let them dry on a low rack for a year. Then he dug long trenches and lined the same with clay, after which he placed each log in a trench and then filled the rest of the trench with the oil. He let the logs float there for two years.

His thinking was that the oil would penetrate into the log making the fibers so slippery that the teredo would be unable to rasp.

"A teflon log."

"Yes. But no one else followed his example. No one wanted to wait so many years before beginning construction. For example, off Tyler Street there once was a huge wharf and at a point in time in 1934 when the owner thought it was stout, it collapsed, due to the pilings becoming hollow due to teredos, and was broken apart by the changing of the tides.

"We actually tested the pilings under the PTMC wharf to see if the diary was truthful. We rowed under the dock on a moonless night and drilled into the pilings and removed core samples, which were sent on to the School of Forestry at the University of Washington. Sure enough, a report came back concluding that the piling fibers were encased in a fishy-smelling oil."

The two men conversed for a while longer and then Michael left. At the motel he attempted to reach Director Bones, but neither he nor Pauline were available. He left a message that he planned to stay two more nights in Port Townsend. He did not reveal that, in a few hours, once it was dark, he planned to break into the old wharf building.

XXI

Back at his motel room, Michael placed the metal barn door handles over pieces of newspaper spread on the balcony floor and he quickly sprayed each handle a brown color. He wanted the handles to be the same color as the exterior wall of the old wharf building. Then he inserted one of the new batteries in the charger and plugged the cord into an electrical wall outlet. To charge one battery would take about an hour and Michael quickly realized there was not enough time to charge all the batteries with one charger. He returned to the hardware store and bought two more chargers. As an afterthought, he also purchased a half-inch drill bit. Now, with three batteries being charged, he'd be ready to go to the old wharf once it became dark. He set his alarm for an hour and then napped until it sounded. Then he removed the charged batteries and waited fifteen minutes before inserting two more batteries. Then he napped for another hour and repeated the process two more times. Chances are he had too many batteries, but he simply did not want the drill, when he was dependent on it, to become useless for want of a usable battery. When the last set of batteries was being charged, he walked to the Bayview Restaurant where, for dinner, he ordered a baked potato and some tea. The restaurant offered a panoramic view of Port Townsend Bay. Waitresses greeted regular customers by their first name. At the counter next to him, to his right, sat a weathered-looking man wearing a black-visored, white-clothed captain's cap. Michael thought he would try to initiate a conversation.

"How's it going?" he asked.

The other fellow kept looking straight ahead, but answered: "OK, how about you?"

"Fine," and then Michael realized here was an opener for forming a conversation, but not being a sports person, he was not certain what to say. He took a chance to see if he might get another reply.

"I took a rowboat out on the bay yesterday and it sure was pleasant."

Mentioning rowboats to anyone in Port Townsend may well be the key to inspire conversation. The other man turned toward Michael and asked what type of rowboat it was. Michael described it as best he could.

"Storm rowing is one of my hobbies," the man said.

"What is that?" Michael half led him on and half wanted to know.

"Well, I paid for some plans for an El Toro sailboat and then I built it as a rowboat. No mast. No well for a centerboard. No seat except in the middle."

"How long is your boat?"

"It's about eight feet long, approximately forty-eight inches wide. The oars I purchased are a foot shorter than normal oars. When Port Townsend Bay gets stormy I put the rowboat in the back of my truck and drive down to the large boat haven. I can row out beyond the jetty right into the storm waves. The boat is like a feather on the water and yet low enough not to be pushed around too much by the wind. Eight feet is just about the right length and the oars, being short, do not catch on the waves."

Michael realized he had opened a gusher. There was no stopping the gentleman next to him from talking about rowboats. Michael wondered if he had mentioned gardening instead of rowboats if the guy would still be silently looking ahead.

"You get out there in a small rowboat like that, middle of a gale, and it is really something. Port Townsend Bay is only two miles across and about six miles long; the waves can only get so big. People on shore start looking at you as though you are crazy, but, really, it is perfectly safe to row an El Toro hull out there in a forty knot wind."

Michael just sat and listened, captive to the very conversation he had kindled.

"Why, one time I was out there and the wind was howling by at fifty knots. The waves were cresting all over the place and the tops of the white caps were blown forward by the wind like one big spray. I thought I was really doing something special being out there—when nearby this local dentist comes along going about 30 miles an hour across the direction of the wind on a sailboard. He was really toot'n. He was there one moment and gone the next, just sailed on by. Imagine standing on a sailboard like that and letting the sail pull you through a storm!"

Michael listened as the man next to him described his former rowboat and then the two before that. There was no way to stop him from talking. As Michael listened he poked at his potato and downed the tea. Finally, the alarm on his cellular phone went bleeping, reminding him to return to the motel to remove the batteries from the charger. He thanked the gentleman next to him for conversing and left. As he neared the motel he looked over at the parking area on the old wharf. No cars were parked there. He checked the float to make certain the rowboat was available. Still daylight, he had time to burn and decided to walk again through downtown. A few doors beyond the hardware store he turned and entered a tavern. The smell of stale beer greeted him. Along a bar men and women sat hunched over. Towards the back of the room amongst some tables a relaxed couple rolled cigarettes and talked. In the middle of the room two women played pool. He walked to the bar and asked for an apple juice. Then he sat alone at a table near the pool table. Some quarters rested in a line on the top ledge of the outer rim of the pool table. Michael noticed that when one player lost, the winner remained at the table and a fellow wearing jeans and a thick leather vest moved from the bar, picked up a quarter and placed it in the slot to start the next game. Michael reached in his pocket and felt a quarter. Casually, he walked over to the pool table and placed his quarter at the end of the line. No one said anything or even looked at him. He had not played pool for years. He closely watched the subsequent games trying to recall the rules.

"This your quarter?"

Michael was a bit apprehensive about playing. Hesitantly he answered affirmatively and walked over to select a cue stick. His opponent stood there watching him. She was short. He noticed lovely blue eyes. "Ellen," she said, "my name is Ellen. Yours?"

"Michael. I'm sort of a tourist here, not much of a pool player. I hope you do not mind playing this game with me."

"No problem."

She must have let up on her skills for Michael actually thought he was winning. People on the bar were no longer looking at the mirror. They were twisting around on their stools, watching the pool game. He had one more ball to pocket before he could sink the eight ball. She had four balls left. Just when he was certain he'd win, she dropped one ball, then the second, then she bounced the cue ball off a cushion to sink a third ball, then down went the fourth, and, almost as fast, the black eight ball rolled into a corner pocket. In one final turn he had lost. She thanked him, and while he walked toward the door she waited by the pool table for the next challenger.

Back at the motel he wrapped his gear in plastic sacks and then placed the same in the rowboat. The clothing he wore was dark-colored, the better to remain unseen. He had no gun.

In darkness he rowed from the motel to the ladder at the old wharf. Once the rowboat was tied to the ladder, he carried one sack up and placed it on the wharf deck. Then he returned to the rowboat and climbed up with a second sack. On the wharf deck he opened one sack and quickly removed the drill. Then he looked for screws and, with a barn door handle in hand, he approached the wooden wall below the broken window. About three feet off the deck he fingered one screw with the same hand that pressed the door handle against the wall, and with his other hand he moved the drill over the head of the square-holed screw and turned on the drill. "EEERRRRUUUUU." In three seconds the screw was deep in the wood and the door handle was ready for three more screws. Quickly Michael drilled in those three screws. Three feet above that handle he secured another. His idea was to reach the window above by climbing the door handles, but once he could no longer stand on the firm footing of the deck, he realized he could not simply stand on a handle for there was nothing to keep his body from falling away from the wall. Necessity being the mother of invention, he found he could unbuckle his belt and wrap it around the barn door handle closest to his waist and then rebuckle it. That way the belt held him to the wall while one foot rested on the handle below. With both hands free he then could screw in the next door handle three feet further up. He knew his leather belt was old and cracked in many places and the higher he went the more he wondered if the belt would hold. When he was fifteen feet above the deck he became very worried about the belt, but kept going.

Finally, his head came to the level of the broken window. He used the body of the drill to press against what glass remained, breaking what was left of the pane of glass and causing the broken pieces to fall into the dark spaces of the attic. Carefully, he pulled a glove from his back pocket and used it to sweep the windowsill free of sharp glass. Then he grabbed the window ledge and pulled himself up. There he balanced, half in the attic and the other half, his legs, pointed out in mid-air. He could see nothing below him. It was just too dark. He moved his hand back to the other back pocket and pulled out a flashlight. His body felt pinched and cramped resting on the window edge. With the beam of the light, he saw inside a floor that consisted of rows of lowered-ceiling joists and on top of the joists rested a line of two by six inch boards, two each, side by side, serving as a catwalk. He lowered the drill as close to the floor as possible and let it drop. "BAAANG!" It landed on a sheet of plasterboard secured below to the joists, and Michael then realized he should have been more careful for the weight of the drill could have broken through the plasterboard ceiling. After the noise, he waited. No alarms sounded. No one stepped out of darkness to grab him. He wiggled and jiggled forward until his body dipped down until his fingers finally touched the top of a joist beam. Then he lowered himself down into the attic. With the use of his flashlight he quickly looked around for pieces of glass that he might otherwise touch or sit on. Then he placed the drill, batteries, screws, and the extra door handles right under the window for safe keeping.

Along the walls of the attic, the flashlight beam showed him rows of windows that had once allowed daylight to brighten the building interior and now were boarded over. The place was dusty. His finger tips were dirty from touching the wood. Black, rice-shaped mice manure lay in abundance on the top of the lowered-ceiling plasterboard. He could see where pigeons roosted. Cloth-covered electrical lines ran between porcelain insulators. Michael guessed the overhead lines were replaced by new wiring in 2004. Slowly, he stepped along the catwalk. Off to one side, his flash-light picked out an object between joists. As he came nearer, he recognized a dead raccoon.

Reality was where he flashed the light. Everything else re-mained invisible in darkness. His light crossed what initially looked like a Chinese lantern hanging from a rafter beam, and on closer inspection he realized it was a large, papery wasp hive. After Michael stepped carefully along the catwalk a good distance through the attic, his light beamed onto a door. He tried the handle. The door did not budge. Impatient, he raised his foot and kicked in a door panel. No alarm sounded. Then he reached through, found a door hook and set it free. With the door opened, he carefully descended narrow wooden steps. Each board creaked when pressed with his weight. There was so much dust there that as he put his feet down an outline of his shoes remained. At the bottom door he waited for any sounds. Hearing nothing, he turned the door handle and the door swung open.

The room he entered was a large kitchen. The clean linoleum floor looked brand new. On one side stood a stainless steel counter and triple sinks. On the walls were cupboards and shelves. To one side were doorways, one to a freezer, the other to a cooler. At the middle of the room rested a large work table. Along one side of that table was a separate steel table that had rollers along its top, like those of a conveyor. At the end of the steel table stood a six-foot tall band saw. Michael realized that the layout was for something to be moved back and forth through the band saw and he thought of the bones below. Just then he noticed next to the band saw the top of a chute. Its walls rose up from the floor to the level of the work table. He raised the chute lid and looked down. When he flashed his light down the chute it reflected back from the surface of the seawater below and it outlined a spider's web. Holding his flashlight close to the web he recognized a brown recluse spider, about the only venomous type of spider in western Washington. Quickly, he replaced the chute lid. Just beyond the wall that had a bank of stoves, ovens and grills, he noticed two swinging doors. One door had words painted on it: "Do not use." The other door was imprinted: "Use this door." Michael walked across the kitchen and pushed on the second door. It swung into a large banquet room. He noticed to his right a wall light switch. When he turned the switch many lights came on. He could see lines of chairs next to rows of dinner tables. At the far end of the room was a raised platform for dignitaries and a master of ceremonies to sit. Just in front of that platform was a separate table that held a three-foot diameter cut-crystal champagne bowl. At one table Michael noticed a stack of papers. He walked over and glanced down. What he saw was the program for the club's annual meeting. At the top it read: "WELCOME TO THE ANNUAL PTMC BANQUET, October 11, 2008."

"That's tomorrow!" Michael realized. He glanced down at the program and learned that dinner began at 6:00 P.M. and that the highlight of the evening, at 8:00, was a dessert of cake and the annual toast of champagne, presumably from the large bowl near the front of the room. Michael folded one of the programs and placed it in his back pocket to read later. He realized that if there were to be a banquet here within 24 hours, people would be arriving soon to do the prep work. He turned off the light and walked back to the kitchen. Worried that people might be coming, he used only his flashlight to look about.

He stopped outside of the walk-in cooler and looked in. The shelves bulged with containers of fresh salad, and stacks of what appeared to be thawing pizza. In the middle of the cooler there was a narrow table on wheels. On the table lay what appeared to Michael to be the torso of a Greek statue, but he immediately recognized the form as that of a headless, limbless, gutted human being.

Just then he heard voices. As the kitchen lights flooded the room with illumination, he jumped into the cooler and closed the door. Over the sounds of the cooler compressor he could hear people talking. And then, when the bright light came on, he realized they were about to enter the cooler. He turned off his flashlight and dropped to the floor. Then he wiggled sideways under a wallshelf. The cooler door swung open. In walked two people.

XXII

"Sweetheart, looks good, doesn't it?"

"Dearest, yes."

Michael could not see what the chummy talk was about, as he was down flat on the cold floor and could not poke his head out for fear of being seen. In front of his face moved polished leather shoes with what looked like new, still-soft socks. The woman's feet were smaller. She wore polished black shoes, nylons, and a black dress that extended down to just above the ankles. He felt cold. He realized he was about to sneeze and pressed a finger across the bottom of his nose to cancel out the urge.

Michael heard the woman say: "Let's see, what is our schedule? First we are to use the band saw to prepare the cakes. Bob and Sue will be here in an hour to set the tables. Then when they finish we will prepare the champagne and decorate the cakes. We should be out of here by four in the morning."

The man answered: "Seems like a tight schedule, but we can do it."

"Yes, love."

"Here, Sweets, if you will please hold the door, I'll roll our dessert out to the center table."

"Sweets!" thought Michael. "They sure use a lot of words of endearment. Maybe their parents never gave them first names."

Michael watched the shoes move. Then he heard the cooler door open and saw the wheels of the table supporting the torso begin to turn. In a moment the door closed and he lay there in darkness. He pushed against the damp wall, moved out from under the shelf, and stood there in darkness. The first thing he did was to use his hands to feel the cooler door. Sure enough, there was an emergency mechanism to open the door from the inside. He felt the wall for a light switch. None. The coldness of the cooler made him uncomfortable but he could not leave. Part of the insulation around the door had been damaged and Michael found that if he put his ear over the crack he could vaguely hear some of the sounds in the next room.

"OK, Precious, push really hard. There. Let it roll onto the cutting table. Good. Now, where is the button for the band saw?"

Then Michael listened to the whirring sounds of the band saw. Repeatedly, the sound changed to a deeper tone, then returned to its higher pitch. Michael guessed that the torso was being pushed back and forth on the conveyor rollers, into the band saw and then back for another cut. By now he was really cold. He sneezed several times and his nose began to run.

"Damn!" Michael heard. Just then the sound of the band saw stopped.

"Blade broke. There is an extra one in the back of the car, I'll go get it. Be right back."

"Fine, darling. While you are gone I'll use the women's room."

Michael realized this was his chance. Waiting briefly, he worked the door lever and leaned against the door. Slowly, very noisily, it opened. As though curious, the outer light flooded in. He stepped out and looked around. The kitchen was empty. His intent was to run to the doorway to the attic steps, but as he glanced about the room, his movement stopped and he stood there staring at the center work area. There he saw a body that looked just like the form he had seen at the morticians' conference. He walked to the center of the room. The torso in front of him had fine black lines running parallel along its length. The body had been run through the band saw. He heard the flushing of a toilet and a door close. He realized the woman would be returning instantly. The attic door was at the far side of the room. There simply was not time to get there.

In a panic he lifted the lid to the chute and lowered himself down. Once inside the chute he pressed his body against the walls to hold his position while he raised his arms to reposition the lid. While his arms were above him he could feel a spider climbing down his arm. The lid would not yet fit properly and, frantically, he kept readjusting it. He recalled seeing the brown recluse spider when he first looked down the chute. That spider moved further along his arm, under his T-shirt. He could feel it moving across his chest and then up his neck to his chin. When it was on his lips, Michael lost control of himself and, maybe by some primitive urge, he decided to destroy the spider by chewing it. He inhaled the spider, drawing it to his back molars, then he chomped down and kept chomping. The spider legs he had felt pricking his gum line stopped. He spit out the dead spider. He did not know if the chute below him had any protruding nails or hooks that might catch his body, but he had little choice except to release his pressure against the chute walls and to fall. A world of cold wetness and unseeable bubbles surrounded him as he sank underwater. When his feet touched bottom his knees bent to lessen the impact and then he straightened his legs, which pushed him toward the surface. He swam to the ladder and climbed it high enough to step into the rowboat.

Back in his motel room he knew he had to sit down and plan for some way to re-enter the wharf building. He wanted to be in the attic to somehow look down to observe the people at the banquet. First he showered and put on some dry clothing. Then he removed from a pocket in his wet pants the banquet program and unfolded it. To his surprise, all the ink had washed free when exposed to saltwater. Nothing remained on the paper that he could read. When he started to shave he looked in the mirror and saw a hair caught between his front teeth. He looked closer. It was not a hair. It was a spider's leg and it was still twitching.

XXIII

For one hour, from three to four o'clock in the morning, Michael slept. When his alarm woke him, he dressed and walked to the front of the motel to see if any vehicles remained parked at the old wharf. None was there; he guessed that the wharf building was empty and would stay that way for another couple of hours. Back in his room he phoned FBI headquarters and again learned that the Director was not available. He probably should have contacted the Seattle FBI office. Arrests would quickly follow. Charges would be filed. The serial murders of single young men would stop. But Michael had another idea. He walked to an all-night store and bought a quart of mineral water. Outside the store he drained the plastic container. Then he walked to where as a child he had sold lemonade. He went up a few of the concrete stairway steps and leaned over to place the container below the run of water that dribbled and seeped down the hillside. Slowly, the container filled. When he held the full container up against the illumination of the street light, he was pleased to see that the water was perfectly clear. He replaced the cap and walked back to the motel.

He could see through the motel room window that the sun would not be too long in coming up. Quickly, he went down to the motel float. It did not take much time to row to the wharf ladder. This time he was careful to place a stern rope around a piling back under the wharf. He tied a loose bow line onto the ladder. He wanted the rowboat to stay under the dock, out of sight as much as possible, and yet he had to allow some slack in the lines to compensate for the changing of the tide.

From the old rusty ladder, he moved to the handles he had screwed to the wall. He ascended to the broken window, balanced himself over the sill, and gently squirmed downward inside the attic to its joist flooring. He felt around below the window and promptly located the drill and his stash of batteries. With his flashlight on so he could see what he was doing, he removed the square drive bit from the drill chuck and widened the chuck opening to allow his half-inch drill to be inserted. When he placed his ear against the attic floor he heard no sounds below. He beamed his light along the catwalk, and as quickly as he could he walked through the attic to the door leading down to the kitchen. The steps creaked. At the bottom door he waited several minutes to listen for the sounds of others. He heard nothing. Slowly, he opened the kitchen door. The room was dark. He used his flashlight to walk to the swinging door. He pushed the door open and reached for the wall light switch and flooded the room with light. Then, quickly, he returned to the attic. Guessing as best he could, he drilled a half-inch hole in the attic ceiling. He bent further over and looked down through the hole in the plasterboard. He could see the tables, all set with plates and eating utensils, but he was ten feet off from the champagne bowl. He moved ten feet and drilled again. This time he could see the champagne bowl about four feet off from directly below him. He drilled again. This time the bowl could be seen directly below the hole. Michael placed the drill where he could find it. Then he quickly returned downstairs. He grabbed the champagne bowl, carried it many feet away, and turned it upside down to dump out the bits of plasterboard debris that had fallen from the drilled hole. Once the bowl was back in place he looked about and brushed and blew telltale white dust off of plates and cups. As he left the banquet room he turned off the lights. In the kitchen he switched on the lights. The work table and the band saw stood there. Nothing rested on the table. The torso was gone. Curious, Michael walked to the cooler, turned on the light and opened the door. On a bank of shelves stood newly placed champagne bottles. To one side the shelves were filled with rows of porcelain saucers that held square cakes. Layered across each cake glistened a covering of chocolate syrup. On the very top, each cake carried a bright red cherry. Michael touched one cake and then put his finger in his mouth. Delicious chocolate. Then he pressed harder against the same cake. His fingernail caught the white substance under the chocolate. Michael sucked on that finger. "Yuck!" It tasted so bland, like unsalted tofu. The texture was not fluffy like cake. Instead it was thick and soft, like soap. He realized the cake was actually pieces of the body he had seen in the cooler and later at the band saw.

Back in the attic he could see daylight coming through the end window. All he could do now was to wait, from morning through the day to early evening when the banquet would begin. He had to be careful where he placed his weight in the attic, for if he stepped on the plasterboard it would break and he would fall through into the banquet room. He moved some of the boards of the catwalk and placed them side by side near the hole above the champagne bowl. Thereby he created a flat place on which to stretch out. Then, using his coat as a pillow, he lay down and went to sleep.

Four hours later, sounds of commotion below woke him. He rolled over and looked down a drill hole. People moved about below him. He could see the tops of the heads of a man and a woman as they walked below carrying bouquets of flowers. They placed the flowers on the head table. "WWRRRRMMMM!" he heard a vacuum cleaner and looked down to see the top of the head of a woman cleaning the floor below. "There goes my dust," he chuckled. Michael wondered if anyone might inspect the attic. He could only hope he stayed undetected for the many hours that remained. He rolled onto his back and went to sleep. Fresh air blew in through the broken window. The ferry whistles and the sounds of unloading and loading vehicles did not bother Michael. A flock of crows flew overhead creating raucous sounds, but not waking Michael. It was not until 6:30 that a "THUMP!! THUMP!! THUMP!! THUMP!! startled him awake. He sat up and looked around, but all he saw was the empty attic.

The sound continued. When he peered through the ceiling hole he saw a person setting up a microphone. To test the volume, the mike was being thumped with the person's hand. The room was filled with well-dressed people. The banquet tables had been serviced, for at each chair rested a plate full of food. A person at the head table jiggled a small bell and everyone sat down and commenced to eat dinner. Michael stared at the champagne bowl. It was almost full. He could see the ceiling lights reflecting off the ice cubes that floated in the champagne. It was time to try his idea. He reached for the plastic bottle that contained the hillside seepage and he removed the lid. Then he tipped the bottle at a very slight angle, just enough to let one drop of water fall through the half-inch hole. It fell down into the banquet room and landed right in the champagne bowl. No one noticed. People kept eating. Slowly, drop by drop, Michael emptied the container.

The bell rang again.

Michael looked down and saw the top of the head of a woman rise from the head table and walk toward the microphone. Then he heard her say:

"Hello, everyone; so good to see you all at the annual meeting of the PTMC. My name is Dorothy Dirtier. Please go on and enjoy your dinner while I talk to you. In a few minutes we will do the annual toast and then have dessert. In the meantime, my wonderful husband, Don Dirtier, will provide a brief history of the PTMC."

"Aha," thought Michael, "now I will learn about this group."

He saw the head of a man rise at the head table and move toward the microphone. He extended his hand to his wife and they shook hands and then they drew each other close and embraced each other tightly. Michael tried to remember some proverb he had once heard about public displays of affection, but he could not put it together.

"Hello. Dorothy and I are so pleased to see you all here. I am sure you all know the background of our group, so I will be brief. All of us are dedicated to the concept of being married. No life is of value without marriage. In our minds, I am sure, we think of marriage as the essence of being an American." He looked toward his wife and Michael could see her smile and her cute blinking as she looked up appreciatively at her spouse.

Michael listened and wondered where this nonsense was going.

Dirtier continued: "Nine years ago, it came to the attention of a group of parents that a teacher at Garfield High School in Seattle taught a social science class in a manner that encouraged children to think twice before getting married. He lectured about the financial difficulties of supporting a family, of the years distracted by screaming babies, and of the alleged fact that so many marriages end in divorce. He even gave the students a statistical projection as to how many of their own children would go to prison. The parents were so alarmed that their kids might never marry and produce grandchildren that they formed a social group to determine a way to prevent that teacher from influencing students. A consensus formed that the easiest way was to kill him. That fall, when he was hunting mountain goats in the Olympic National Forest, members of the group intercepted him and pushed him off a cliff in a manner that looked accidental. Thereafter the group increased in number and became dedicated to searching out, within the educational system of the public schools of our country, single men who advocate to the students that they remain single. Many of you here tonight were part of that first social group. As you know, the club is divided into six sections. One section searches for wayward teachers. Another section intercepts and eliminates such teachers. A third section manages the club properties. A fourth section, which this year includes me and my lovely wife, Dorothy, prepares the annual banquet. The fifth section is responsible for keeping track of bodies as they chemically change on the bottom of Lake Crescent. The sixth section has a year off—and then at the end of the year all the sections rotate. I think I have talked long enough and now return the microphone to the gracious lady of my life, my wife, Dorothy."

"Well, hi, I'm back. So many of you have driven a long way to be here. I'll bet you are tired. How about taking a break right now and simply standing and embracing your loved one?"

Michael could see chairs being pushed back from the tables. Then he saw couples wrapping their arms around each other, hugging and kissing. A chorus of "MMMMMMMMMMM" sounds reached him as the people smooched. Something about organized affection bothered him and he thought the people below looked ridiculous.

"Oh, wasn't that wonderful?" bantered Dorothy Dirtier into the microphone. "Now, please, will each table send a delegate to the front of the room to get a glass pitcher and then proceed to the champagne bowl to have the pitcher filled. Back at your tables, please fill each person's cup in preparation for the annual toast."

At the same time, Michael saw people coming from the kitchen with trays that contained the cake. The cakes were placed, one by one, in front of each person. Soon, glasses of champagne and saucers of dessert cake rested side by side throughout the banquet room.

Dorothy Dirtier continued. "Now, my friends, before eating the dessert, please stand with me now, raise your champagne, let me lead you in our annual toast."

Michael saw rows of heads rising toward him and then rows of champagne glasses lifted up in his direction. "Ladies and gentlemen, here is our toast to marriage: Let no one prevent marriage. To marriage!"

The crowd repeated her. "To marriage. Let no one prevent marriage. To marriage." The toast and the response were repeated two more times.

Michael carefully watched as the champagne glasses tilted toward the respective holders and then drained. Below him, the people at the banquet sat down and began to eat the dessert.

The room was quiet as the people munched. Occasionally, someone picked a large bone from the cake and pushed it with a fork to the side of the plate. Michael realized that those bones would later be dropped down the chute and added to the underwater mound. He watched closely, thinking something might happen. But nothing took place. The people just sat there, hunched over the table, eating bits and pieces of chocolate-smothered dessert.

XXIV

Down through the drilled hole in the ceiling Michael kept looking. He observed people, rows of people, munching on cake. No one spoke. The entire banquet room remained quiet. Everything appeared orderly. In a while the people would leave, disappear. Slowly Michael realized that his plan was foolish, that he had made a terrible mistake of judgment. The stairway seepage water he added to the champagne was just that: water. Nothing more. What an idiot he had been. It was too late to call for the building to be surrounded. He could imagine the anger of Director Bones and his own sense of embarrassment at a future point in time when he had to file an official report. The press would have a field day. Congress will send a subpoena to humiliate him. He'll be fired. Most of the killers below would escape detection.

His arms ached from holding the upper body over the drill hole. He decided to sit up to give his arms a rest. As he braced to lift himself he noticed below the hand of a lady go over her dinner plate and grab a large serving fork. The way she grabbed it was odd. Rather than hold it as though to serve food, she held it with her thumb at the end of the implement handle. Michael kept watching. She rose from her chair, raised her hand with the fork up toward Michael—and he could see the long, sharp double spikes of the fork tines—and then she turned toward the man next to her who had remained seated and her hand swung into an overhead arc. She plunged the fork into the soft part of the gentleman's skull and the fork, up to its handle, disappeared into the brain. He slumped forward over the remaining half of his cake, dead, with a fork handle visible in the middle of his bald spot.

"Wow!" exclaimed Michael. People started to push each other.

The room remained quiet no longer. He heard angry comments, banging sounds and then screams. Then, directly below him, he saw Don Dirtier circle his arms around his wife Dorothy. She screamed in protest as he lifted her up, turned her upside down and placed her face down in the champagne bowl. For a moment her legs flutter-kicked as though she were doing the Australian crawl. Then the legs moved slower and slower until she drowned. He lowered her to the floor and put his hands overhead and yelled "Yes!"

At one dining area the people on one side had pushed the long table over on top of the eaters on the other side, and Michael saw people jumping up and down on the overturned table. One woman swung a small fork into the forehead of her husband. He reached forward toward her, the fork still stuck to his skull, placed his fingers around her neck, and cut off her air supply. Michael saw a lady reach down below her chair and remove a spiked heel. She placed the palm of her right hand onto the back top of the shoe and turned toward the man next to her. She plunged the tip of the heel into his eye socket, the shoe heel being so long it penetrated his brain. With the shoe stuck to him, he fell over backwards, dead. Michael forgot the discomfort of his arms. A riot, a melee, was underway below him. Bodies began to fall and twitch on the floor. Heavy plates, thick ceramic platters and bowls of food, tossed, sometimes hit an intended target, usually just crashed down on the floor. Suddenly, one side of the room consisted of women and the other of men. Each side yelled at the other and raised fists in rage. "I hate you! Die dog! You've ruined my life! Pig!" were some of the remarks that rose up and passed through the ceiling drill hole to Michael's ears. From both sides he heard the beginnings of a chant: "Marriage sucks! You suck! Marriage sucks! You suck!" repeatedly. At the height of the yelling and gesturing, the two sides reached a level of anger where each person no longer thought of his or her own safety, and the two sides rushed at each other. To his horror, Michael saw three women with a heavy paper cutter. They held a man down and forced his fingers onto the cutting platform, then they pressed down the heavy steel arm. When he was fingerless, two sat on him and the third placed the cutter platform under his head and then jumped onto the blade. His head rolled away, staring briefly, half-turned, up at Michael.

In the kitchen, two couples were working. They had missed the annual toast. A blender's whirring sounds barred noise of the turmoil in the banquet room from reaching their ears. One of the four, out of curiosity, opened the door leading to the steps to the attic. She saw the footprints on the dusty steps. Slowly, she climbed the steps and looked down the long attic way. The light from the end window beamed in on Michael's back. Realizing someone was spying on the room below, she hurried downstairs and told the other three.

Slowly, one by one, they ascended the steps and walked the catwalk until they stood behind Michael. Each held a meat cutting knife. "Stand, hold out your wrists," one commanded. Michael, totally surprised, rose to his feet. He wanted to run for the window, but it would take too much time to get out. He could step onto the plasterboard and disappear, but the twenty-foot drop into the whirl of the dining room would be most harmful. Slowly, he raised his hands to his belt level and brought them together. A man circled cotton string several times around his wrists. Then they pushed him along the catwalk, down the attic steps, and forced him on top of the work table right in front of the band saw.

"Help!" he yelled. "Help! Stop!" Added to the sound of the blender was the high-pitched tone of the band saw.

"Mildred," one of them said, "please take the lid off the chute. This here gentleman is truly 'going to pieces.'" Mildred took the chute lid and placed it under the table where Michael lay.

"Stop!" he yelled again. "FBI! You are all under arrest! Put your hands up!"

The four people started laughing at him and placed hands onto Michael's body. He could feel his body being pushed over the conveyor rollers toward the band saw. Hundreds of sharp metal cutting teeth circled just above his head. A saw tooth caught on his hair and ripped out a patch of his hair. Just then, they realized that his clothing would cause the saw blade to snag on the fibers, so they pulled Michael back, removed his clothing, and then recommenced to push him toward the saw. Michael realized he was a goner. He looked around the room for help, but it was empty, except for two well-dressed couples approaching from the direction of the parking area. "What a way to die," he thought, "pieces of FBI crab food."

He looked up. Four smirking faces peered down, each eager to push his body into the saw. He could see them balance backwards in order to lurch forward to press him through the blade. A smell— his olfactory senses alerted Michael to a new smell. He had encountered that smell many times before. "What is it?" he asked himself. Marijuana. He smelled marijuana. The same smell that punctuated the air at FBI headquarters. Then, seeming to him as though he were dreaming, "Turn off the saw!" he heard Director Richardson Bones yell. Michael knew he was just dreaming; wishful thinking in the very last stage of his life. The saw kept turning and hands still pushed against his body.

"BLAM! BLAM! BLAM! BLAM!" Hand pressure on his body stopped. The four around him fell to the floor. Fingers came forward and pressed the "off" button on the band saw. Michael looked up and recognized Pauline in a formal gown. Next to her in a tuxedo stood FBI Director Richardson Bones. Bones' mouth was wide open and he was staring at the other man, also in a tuxedo.

"Benny, was that necessary; did you have to shoot?"

"Yes," thought Michael. When Pauline turned off the blender they could hear the sounds of screaming, yelling, and fighting in the banquet room.

"What is that?" asked Bones.

"They are trying to kill each other."

"Why?"

"I spiked their drink."

"You what? Why?"

"These people captured and killed the young men. Some sort of demented hatred for people who advocate staying single."

"Say what?" remarked the FBI Director. "What are we going to do now? Whoever these people are, they are entitled to due process, to a fair trial. We can't just poison them and shoot them. Congress will have a party interrogating us before we go to prison. What are we going to do?" The string on Michael's wrists was cut. He scrambled for his clothing.

Director Bones did not see Benny whisper to his wife. She went and took a candle and a cup from a counter and then she walked to the side of the room away from the gas ovens. She lit the candle and rested it inside the cup. She placed the cup and the candle on a cabinet shelf and left the cabinet door just slightly ajar. Then Benny walked to the ovens. Quickly, he manipulated the pilot lights so that gas could pass even though the pilot lights were off. Then at each stove he turned the gas on full. A hissing sound came to the Director's ears. He looked at the stoves. He guessed what Benny and his wife had done.

"Stop this!" he commanded. "Illegal! This is clearly illegal!"

"You do remember your dog?" Benny said. "Do you recall that after I went out on the ice and saved your dog, you said you owed me a favor? This is it. These people killed Gudrun's and my son. Now, Rich, the favor you promised is being called."

Bones did not know what to do. He looked about the room, knew it was filling with gas. He stood there uncertain. Then in a spark of energy he exclaimed: "We're out of here!" They ran for the door leading to the parking lot. Reaching the car, Bones turned the ignition key. Their car rolled off the old wharf dock, wheeled by the motel, and headed for the airport. Michael slumped in the back seat. He thanked the others for saving his life. The Director commented that chances are someone entered the kitchen and turned off the gas. The speed limit, twenty-five miles an hour, kept their car at a slow pace. Bones did not want a police car stopping them on account of speeding. He wanted anonymity.

Suddenly, as their car approached the bottom curve of Sims

Way on Highway 20, through Michael's open window entered the sound of one huge explosion. Benny looked back, saw a glow of flames above where the wharf would be. He turned to his wife and told her that he thought the fire from the explosion would burn down the entire wharf.

Bones radioed ahead. At the airport an FBI plane waited. As the plane took off, Gudrun faced Michael and asked where her son's body was. Michael explained that as best he could figure it rested at the bottom of Lake Crescent. Bones told her the FBI would send a diving team to look. When the plane reached an elevation of 2,000 feet, the Director asked the pilot to circle back to Port Townsend but to keep the plane at last one-half mile east. From the plane windows they looked down. Flames licked up hundreds of feet. The entire shoreline was illuminated. Along Water Street red lights flashed from fire trucks and blue lights disclosed the presence of many police cars. Intense heat kept the firemen at a distance from the old wharf. They used their equipment to hose down the motel and the building on the other side of the old wharf. The gas tank in one car parked on the old wharf exploded, then another, then all of the cars parked there were aflame. Benny commented, "That is quite a fire. Must be a lot of dry wood in the structure." Michael related what he had learned about the fish oil being impregnated into the pilings.

"Let's away," instructed Bones to the pilot, and the plane banked east. At Seattle, they transferred to another FBI plane that had the capacity to fly all the way to Denver and then on to DC. Pauline fell asleep. Bones smoked a joint. Michael stared out the window, watching as the plane passed over tiny lights below—sometimes lights of a small town, of a road intersection, yard lights for farms, and once in a while auto headlights shining on the roadway. In the plane Benny and Gudrun's overhead lights were on. They were playing cribbage. Director Bones leaned toward Michael. "Say, tell me please, just what does PTMC stand for?" Michael replied he did not know.

Just then, they heard Gudrun yell at Benny: "You dim bulb! You low level farm animal! You creep! You are cheating!"

Benny chuckled at his wife's anger and replied: "I'm not cheating. You are just so vain you cannot recognize my skill at cribbage."

"You are cheating! I'm cutting you off from coffee!"

Benny looked at her and said, "Stop postponing your obvious defeat. Just deal the cards."

She dealt and he quickly examined his cards. "I do not want you cheating anymore. If you cheat, the barn is your new home," she muttered.

Bones and Michael had heard them arguing. Bones said to Michael: "Looks like an excellent marriage to me. What do you think?"

Michael replied, "The best."

The end.